chocolate heart murder

A Maple Hills Cozy Mystery - 10

wendy meadows

Majestic Owl Publishing LLC
P.O. Box 997
Newport, NH 03773

❀ Created with Vellum

The small town of Maple Hills was being transformed into a winter wonderland of love. Valentine's Day was approaching, and Nikki watched as the gazebo on the town green was decorated for this very special occasion, with garlands of glittering snowflakes and hearts all around. However, this would not be just an ordinary event, because the mayor's daughter was getting married on Valentine's Day, and in the small town of Maple Hills that counted as a special holiday. Nikki smiled as she watched the workers climb ladders to string lights around the park. The wedding was a week away, and it was the talk of the town. Everyone was excited and happy for the mayor's daughter. Maple Hills was a small town with a strong community where everyone watched out for each other, which was exactly why Nikki liked the town so much. Coming from the big city of Atlanta, it was nice to live in a cozy town.

Nikki looked around her chocolate shop with a smile. The shop was decorated for Valentine's Day, much like the rest of Maple Hills. There were red hearts covering the walls and small dishes of sample chocolate hearts throughout the store. Nikki had even created a special drink, red velvet hot chocolate, just for the holiday. Her customers were enjoying a taste of the south in this cold, snowy winter. Valentine's Day was always a busy time of year for chocolatiers, and this year was no exception. Nikki had a reliable base of local customers that had grown to include people from neighboring towns, and it was even busier this season, especially since Nikki had won a popular chocolate competition. Nikki had a reputation for making good chocolates that tasted so good you knew they came from the heart. She put her soul into her confections, and it showed.

Nikki turned from the window to help the next customer. Mrs. Handle, an elderly and sweet woman, was taking her time deciding which chocolates would be best for her husband. She finally picked out a half pound of white chocolate truffles and bonbons, and Nikki arranged them in a box and wrapped it in red tissue paper with white hearts. Mrs. Handle thanked her and turned to leave. Just then the door opened, and the mayor's daughter came walking in. She held the door for Mrs. Handle and walked up to the counter where Nikki was placing some more striped mint chocolates in the gleaming display case.

"Hello, Susan," Nikki said with a smile as the young woman approached the counter.

"Hello, Ms. Bates," Susan replied. "You look busy today."

"Yes, I'm getting ready for Valentine's Day. It is one of the busiest times of the year for me," she replied.

"Could I take a moment of your time to talk with you?" asked Susan.

Nikki readily agreed and motioned to a table nearby. Susan was in her early thirties, tall and dark-haired, and always walked confidently into a room. Her wedding was the event the town had been buzzing about for a month, but she never seemed to let the attention go to her head. Susan was not a regular customer, but she would occasionally get some hot chocolate to go. Nikki wiped her hands on her apron. On the spur of the moment, Nikki poured Susan some of the red velvet hot chocolate. "Try this, it will help soothe your nerves," Nikki said with a sympathetic smile. She gave Susan the hot chocolate and sat across from her.

"Oh, thank you, Nikki. This is perfect," Susan said after sipping the chocolate. Her face lit up, and she smiled. Nikki could see the stress melting away, at least for now.

"You're welcome," said Nikki. "You must be stressed with all the planning."

"Yes. You might have noticed that there have been just a few decorations going up in the park," Susan said with a twinkle in her eye. "I am so excited about getting married, and I want every detail to be perfect. You have the best chocolates around, and I was hoping I could get you to have a table at my reception. If it's not too late, that is," she added hastily. She continued, seeing the encouraging smile on Nikki's face. "I was hoping for some special chocolates and a chocolate fountain. This hot chocolate is wonderful, but I do not suppose a hot chocolate fountain would be practical."

"I would love to set up a table with some of my chocolates and a chocolate fountain for you. And no, I would not recommend hot chocolate; however, you are welcome to come in anytime this week and get some of the special Valentine's Day hot chocolate on the house to try," Nikki replied. She was excited, but her mind was racing as she started planning how to make this work on top of the extra batches of special chocolates she was already making for Valentine's Day.

"Thank you, Ms. Bates. I appreciate you being willing to do this so last-minute."

"I am happy to help you have the perfect day," Nikki replied.

"Also, please consider this an invitation to the wedding. I hope you and your staff will also be able to make it."

"I wouldn't miss it," Nikki replied.

Susan thanked her again and stood up to leave. "Oh, those

strawberries look scrumptious. I'll take a dozen of them." Nikki had crafted delectable chocolate-covered strawberries for Valentine's Day. They were a hit with her customers.

Nikki got up and boxed the strawberries for Susan. Susan paid for the chocolates, thanked Nikki, and left, the bell on the door tinkling behind her. As soon as she had gone, Lidia finished with another customer and then walked over to the table. Lidia was Nikki's trusted partner and assistant who helped run the shop and make the chocolates. She was an older woman with a strong work ethic. Nikki appreciated having her around.

"What did Susan want to talk about?" Lidia asked, intrigued. They walked back to the kitchen together.

"Susan would like a table of chocolates and a chocolate fountain at her wedding. I told her I would make it happen, and now I need to figure out what kinds of chocolates I'm going to make for her." Nikki sat down at the work table in the kitchen and Lidia joined her.

"Well, we already have the strawberries – maybe you could do a special batch of those?" Lidia suggested.

"That's a good start," replied Nikki. "We could also dip some other fruit in chocolate. That would make a pretty arrangement."

"Should I order some oranges and grapefruits so we can get started?" Lidia asked.

"Not yet. Let's figure out what else we are going to do and run it by Susan first," said Nikki. They talked a bit and came up with a plan. Nikki called Susan. She explained the menu to her.

"I thought we would create some chocolate-dipped fruit and other fruit candies and have a chocolate fountain with different items to dip," Nikki told Susan.

"That is a great idea," Susan said excitedly. "I already tried the strawberries on my way home, I couldn't resist! They were amazing. Thank you again for getting this together so quickly. When you make the chocolate-dipped fruits, can it include our wedding colors somehow?"

Nikki was certain she could make it work, and they worked out the final details in no time at all. "I'll get on this right away," promised Nikki.

When Nikki got off the phone, she made a list. "There's no time for us to place an order through our usual produce supplier, Lidia. We'll have to get everything from the grocery store, I suppose." Lidia was excited by the challenge of helping to craft the elegant candies and chocolates for the display, and quickly left for the store.

How am I going to get everything done? Nikki thought for a moment and picked up her cell phone again. *I'll give Hawk a call. He'll be able to help me.* Hawk was a local detective who occasionally helped Nikki at the store. She also helped him with his investigations. It worked out well. He was tall, dark, and handsome, and his heart belonged to Nikki.

"Hey, Hawk, do you have a minute?"

"Anything for you, Nikki," Hawk replied sweetly into the phone.

"Susan stopped by today and asked me to set up a table for her wedding. Lidia offered to do the shopping, and I have Seth and Tori here to help; however, I could use an extra set of hands this week. Is there any chance you could give me a hand?"

"I would be happy to," Hawk answered.

"Okay, great! Could you stop by the shop after work tonight?" Nikki asked.

"Absolutely. Do you want me to bring some dinner?"

"That sounds good. I might be here all night," Nikki said with a sigh.

"I'll stop by the diner first. Will everyone else be there?"

"I think they will, since this is a last-minute order. I hate to have them stay late, especially if they have plans. I will run it by Seth and Tori, but they already knew this week would be busy."

"I'll bring enough for everyone."

"You don't have to do that, Hawk."

"I know, but I want to. Someone has to keep you and your crew fed."

"Thank you. I'll see you later tonight."

Nikki hung up and headed to the front of the shop to talk to Seth and Tori. Nikki's son Seth was home for February break from college, and she was grateful for his help in the shop since he knew many of her recipes by heart. Nikki's marriage to Seth's father had ended many years ago, and after her husband left, Nikki brought Seth to Maple Hills for a fresh start. Tori, Nikki's employee, was the same age as Seth. They had fallen in love over the past couple months and Nikki could not be happier.

Tori and Seth were just finishing up with some customers. When they were done, Nikki asked them if they would be willing to stay late that night. She told them about Susan's wedding plans.

"A chocolate fountain?" Tori asked. "That sounds delicious."

"What are we going to serve with it?" asked Seth.

"Lidia and I thought we could provide marshmallows, rice crispy squares, angel food cake, caramels, and pretzel sticks."

"That sounds so good," Tori said. "You're making me hungry!"

"Lidia is already at the grocery store picking up supplies, so we need to finish up the store orders for today and tomorrow so that we can start working on the wedding chocolates as soon as possible."

"What are you going to do with the fruit and chocolate?" Tori asked.

"I think I will dip them in white chocolate and decorate

them with a pink swirl," Nikki decided, thinking back to her conversation with Susan about the wedding colors.

"That sounds pretty," Lidia said, coming in with the groceries.

"Okay, so how many more trays do we need to make tonight to complete the store orders?" Nikki asked Tori. Tori went to the clipboard by the register and totaled up the orders.

"It looks like we need at least thirty to cover the special orders."

"Plus regular customer traffic, plus Valentine's Day traffic…I think fifty trays should cover it," Nikki said.

"I can always make more tomorrow if you need me to," suggested Seth. Nikki flashed a grateful smile to her son, and then she delegated tasks to everyone. The front doorbell sounded, and Nikki poked her head out of the kitchen to greet a customer who had just walked in from the cold. Tori offered to take care of them while Nikki and the others got to work. Lidia began preparing oranges and grapefruits, some of which would be dried and candied, while Nikki began melting chocolate on the stove in a large copper kettle. The rich smells drifted out from the kitchen, making the shop smell even more amazing than usual.

Other customers followed soon after that, and Tori cheerfully helped them pick out some Valentine's Day chocolates, ducking back into the kitchen to help in between customers. Occasionally, Seth would join her at the register if there was a long line. They both worked together well, and all the customers left happy. Nikki knew when the local schools let out because the shop would become crowded with teenagers buying chocolates for their boyfriends and girlfriends. Others would sit together at a corner table and study while sipping hot chocolate. Nikki did not mind. Students were quiet, courteous, and very reliable customers.

As the day went on, Tori and Seth were worn out by closing time.

By the time the shop closed, Nikki was putting the finishing touches on the last of the twenty trays she and Lidia had completed. Just as she placed the last tray of pink chocolate roses on the drying rack, Hawk appeared with the food, and everyone stopped to eat. He had brought burgers and fries from the local diner for everyone. Nikki was famished, and she knew her crew would be too. She gave Hawk a hug and kiss and thanked him for bringing the food. Everyone sat around the table in the break room with their burgers and fries, happy for the food and for the brief rest after such a busy day.

As Seth and Tori cleared up the dinner, Hawk looked back into the kitchen with interest. "How many trays do you have left?" Hawk asked Nikki.

"About thirty," Nikki said with a sigh, wiping her hands on her apron. "We should be able to work faster now that the shop is closed."

"And now that you have an extra set of hands," Hawk offered with a smile.

"Thank you…but are you sure I'm not taking you away from anything else?" Nikki asked.

"Of course not," Hawk replied. "There is nowhere else I would rather be." He kissed Nikki, and they went to work. Since Lidia and Nikki had prepared trays of bonbons and truffles earlier that afternoon, it was time to make the chocolate-dipped strawberries. Hawk and Seth set up by the sink and prepped the strawberries. Tori prepared the different dipping chocolates and was in charge of dipping them, and then Lidia and Nikki decorated each berry with swirls and stripes of contrasting color. After a few hours, the last tray was finally done.

"They look amazing," Tori said, stepping back to admire

their work. On the wide work counter sat trays and trays of white, dark, and milk chocolate-dipped strawberries.

"Let's get them in the refrigerator and call it a night," suggested Nikki. While she and Lidia had been finishing the decorating, Tori and Seth had gone up front to take care of the closing tasks while Hawk pitched in to clean the last few pots and utensils. Everyone was tired but satisfied, and they put the chocolates away. Nikki turned off the light and locked the store. Everyone went home to get some rest before they tackled the wedding chocolates the next day. Nikki said goodnight to Hawk, and Seth walked Tori to her car. He lingered at Tori's car door when Nikki called to him that it was time to go, talking to the young woman through her rolled-down window. After a moment more, he reluctantly turned to join his mother.

Nikki and Seth rode home, chatting about how satisfied they were with what they had accomplished that day. Nikki asked Seth if he minded working over break.

"Of course not," he replied. "I want to help make sure this business is a success."

"Is that the only reason?" Nikki teased.

"Okay," he grinned, "I would be in the shop anyway, distracting Tori. This way you get an extra set of hands, and I get to spend the day with my girlfriend. This is winning all around."

Nikki laughed as she drove them home through the sleepy neighborhoods, happy that her stress was from too much work and not from too little.

chapter two

The next morning, Nikki and Seth were up early to drive back to the shop. They met Tori and Lidia in the back parking lot, Tori stifling a yawn as she greeted Seth with a smile. Nikki opened the door to the shop, excited to start the day. As she turned on the lights and started up the hot chocolate machine, she knew her customers would want to come in and get warm on such a cold day. Tori, Seth, and Lidia were busy fetching chocolates out of the refrigerator as they started boxing orders for customers that would be delivered or picked up that day. Nikki set up the display cases, putting out some of the freshly-made pink chocolate roses, and unlocked the front door. It was early, but plenty of people came in for a hot chocolate or a coffee in the morning, and it seemed today would be no exception.

"Nikki, we've got plenty of hands up front to finish these customer orders and manage the shop. Don't worry about us," Lidia reassured her, shooing her back towards the kitchen. Nikki shot her trusted assistant a grateful smile and went back to the kitchen to work on the wedding chocolates.

Nikki could hear the bell at the front door ringing almost constantly and was happy that people were already coming in and business was so brisk. She wanted to jump in to help, but she knew that the others could handle the work just fine on their own.

Nikki consulted her notes from Susan's order, then looked around the kitchen and laid out her ingredients. Lidia had already prepared one batch of citrus fruits for candying, which meant it was now time to work on the chocolate-dipped citrus. Nikki peeled the oranges and grapefruits and divided them into wedges. She worked carefully to remove the bitter pith from each slice, thinking about Susan's wedding and how every detail should be perfect. When Nikki was satisfied with the array of fruit slices before her, she melted white chocolate in a small copper saucepan on the stove until it turned into a glossy, tempered dip. She dipped half of the citrus fruit into the fragrant white chocolate, using a set of special dipping tools to cradle the fruit gently as she set them to dry on a sheet of wax paper. Nikki spent all morning working on the white chocolate fruits, and then switched to milk chocolate. Seth and Tori would occasionally pop in and help as they could, but the store had a steady stream of customers. Lidia remained in the back with Nikki once the milk chocolate was tempered and ready for dipping because they had to work quickly. Together they each dipped the fruits into the chocolate, steadily covering the trays, while Tori and Seth took care of the customers out front.

Around noon, Hawk walked in the front door of the shop and greeted Seth with a big smile. Seth informed him that Nikki was in the back, and Hawk hurried to find her. He saw her dipping a piece of grapefruit in dark chocolate and came up behind her. He put his arms around her and gave her a hug.

"How is everything coming along?" Hawk asked.

"It is moving along," Nikki said while placing the last fruit wedge on the tray. She tested one of the milk chocolate-dipped fruits. "These ones are done drying. Can you help me put them in the refrigerator?" she asked Hawk.

Hawk agreed and picked up two trays and followed her to the refrigerators. They placed them in the refrigerator that was now dedicated only to the wedding job, and which was starting to look a little full. Hawk asked Nikki if she had time for lunch. Lidia, who was washing up at the sink, overheard and insisted that she go and take a break. "Besides, I have to check on the fruits I prepared yesterday and start the candying process. Plus, we are right on schedule with the preparations." Nikki hesitated and then shrugged. Perhaps her friend was right.

"Okay. Those chocolates need to set for a while and harden. I suppose I can start on the cakes and rice crispy squares after lunch."

"Good. I was hoping to get some time alone with you," Hawk said as he held Nikki's coat open for her. Nikki smiled up at his gentlemanly gesture as she donned her hat, scarf, and gloves. She and Hawk walked out of the shop holding hands.

There was snow falling gently outside. It made the town sparkle. Having moved from Atlanta, Nikki was still getting used to snow. She thought it was beautiful, though. As she and Hawk strolled down the sidewalk, they looked into the shop windows, which were decorated with hearts and cupids. Nikki admired an antique roll-top desk, and Hawk looked at some antique guns displayed in the window of the town's most popular antique shop. A glint caught Nikki's eye, and she bent closer to the window.

"Did you see something you like?"

"There's an old locket." She looked closer, marveling that it had caught her eye amid the old glasses, antique fountain pens, and knick-knacks displayed on the desk.

"It's nice," Hawk commented, following her gaze.

"Beautiful." The locket was pale gold with engraved flowers and a little diamond at the clasp. "It reminds me of a locket that my father gave my mother, a long time ago."

They continued down the street. Hawk and Nikki looked through the bookstore window and waved to the owner. Hawk asked Nikki if she wanted to stop inside, but Nikki declined with a smile.

"I have so much to do today. If I stop in a bookstore I will not come out for two hours at least," Nikki laughed.

They finally reached the diner and sat in a small booth by the windows, enjoying the view of the sparkling winter landscape outside. Hawk ordered a burger and fries, and Nikki had a chicken sandwich with onion rings. As they ate their lunch, the owner came over and talked to them for a while. He asked Nikki to hold a dozen chocolate-covered strawberries for him as a surprise for his wife. Nikki agreed.

"What's that impish smile all about?" Hawk inquired, seeing her look.

"What he doesn't know is that his wife stopped in the other day and got a box for him. They will both be surprised on Valentine's Day," Nikki whispered across the table.

Hawk took a sip of his coffee and shook his head at her. "You're a regular cupid, Nikki."

"That's one of the best parts of owning a chocolate shop this time of year. I get to know all the secrets people are planning for their sweethearts!"

Nikki and Hawk sat and ate their lunch. The food was delicious and filled Nikki up. It was not heavy enough to make her tired, and Nikki was grateful for that. If she lost focus now, the chocolates would never get done. When they finished their lunch, Hawk paid the bill despite Nikki's protests, and then they sat and finished their coffee together. Hawk watched Nikki drink and was content to sit there quietly, enjoying her company and the quiet background noise of the diner's kitchen at work.

It was not often Nikki found someone like Hawk. Most people liked to talk all the time, but Hawk was comfortable just sitting in quiet contemplation. Sometimes his quiet contemplation was just what Nikki needed. Nikki could feel her stress melting away while she sat with Hawk. Nikki enjoyed being with Hawk. He was a fun, sweet person. They had grown closer, and she was glad he was in her life. He had helped her out this past year with her shop, and she had even helped him solve some of his cases. This was why they were such an interesting match, she thought to herself.

Years before, Nikki was supposed to go to the FBI Academy at Quantico but was forced to give up her place because of her ex-husband. Her father had been in the FBI, and she liked to joke that he trained her from the time she could walk. He taught her everything he knew and what she had learned from him had helped her solve crimes with Hawk. She and Hawk had even worked on some cases involving her and Seth, unfortunately. Luckily, everything had turned out fine in the end. She felt lucky to be able to share her life-long love of crime solving with this wonderful, caring man who sat across from her at the diner right now.

It had been a quiet winter since Christmas, and Nikki was enjoying just running the shop. She and Hawk relaxed for a while longer before they walked back to the chocolate shop, hand in hand. She took comfort from his quiet strength and understanding. The snow was still falling, and some blew in around their shoulders when they opened the door of the shop.

The shop was busy, but Tori and Seth had it under control. The customers who were waiting looked patient, and Nikki was happy for that. She was turning to say goodbye to Hawk when someone pulled her elbow. Nikki turned and saw the mayor standing in front of her. He wore heavy winter boots over his suit and a heavy coat. He smiled.

"Nikki, I was looking for you. It is good to see you."

"You too, Mr. Mayor," Nikki replied. "Would you like to sit down with us?" She looked at Hawk, and he rolled his eyes. She knew it would be better if they were together to talk to the mayor. He was a respected man, but he was also an older gentleman who could ramble at times.

"Yes, that would be fine," the mayor replied. Nikki, Hawk, and the mayor sat at a table in the corner. Seth had told Lidia that the mayor was there and so she had gotten some hot chocolate for him. The mayor sipped his hot chocolate and asked Nikki what she had planned for her chocolate table. Nikki described the chocolates she was making, and the mayor's eyes lit up when she mentioned the chocolate fountain.

"I don't think I need to remind you how special this day is for me and my wife. My baby girl is getting married, and I want everything to be perfect. There will be many important people at the wedding, and they can make or break a person's business. I hope your chocolates will be perfect," the mayor said with a knowing look.

"They will be," interrupted Hawk. "Don't forget, Nikki won the chocolate competition in December. Her chocolates are always delicious."

"I am sure they will be," said the mayor. He shook their hands and left the shop. Nikki was pleasantly surprised by his short visit. *I suppose he is busy getting things organized too,* she thought.

Nikki thanked Hawk again for the lunch as he left, and then returned to the kitchen. After she washed her hands and tied her apron's strings just right, Nikki knew she was ready for the angel food cake. She prepared her baking table first, setting out flour, sugar, and salt next to a large mixing bowl and sifter, and then took out a tray of thirty-six eggs and set it down next to her electric mixer. She started sifting the dry ingredients for the angel food cake, humming under her breath as she measured and poured. Then she cracked open eggs, separating the yolks into one bowl and the whites into another, until the egg tray was nothing but shells. While the electric mixer whipped the egg whites, she prepared three

Bundt pans. She lined them with parchment paper and then checked that the oven was heating correctly. The egg whites were standing up in stiff, perfect peaks when she checked the mixer, so she carefully folded the egg whites and the dry ingredients together, using two large spatulas. As a final touch, she fetched vanilla and almond extracts from her special shelf of flavorings and added them to the batter until it smelled just right. Carefully, she poured the batter into the prepared pans, and then she shook each Bundt pan a little bit, letting any bubbles rise to the surface and pop. After they were in the oven, Nikki finally gave a sigh of relief.

Next, she planned on making the rice crispy treats. As she carried her mixing bowls to the sink, Lidia peeked through the doorway. "What is that heavenly smell?"

"I just put in the angel food cakes," Nikki responded. "Do we have enough chocolates for the store for the rest of the day?" Lidia assured her that they did and suggested they make some more the next day. Nikki was relieved to know she could continue her wedding prep and started gathering the ingredients for the rice crispy squares.

"Just let me know if you need anything, Nikki," Lidia said, and then headed back to the front of the store to help Seth and Tori.

As the afternoon wore on, Nikki was still working in the kitchen. She kept an organized kitchen, which helped when she had large orders. She flew around preparing her ingredients and tools. The staff knew just where to put things, so Nikki did not have to waste her time looking. After she checked the cakes in the oven, Nikki melted marshmallows in a massive kettle on the stovetop and mixed in the crispy cereal. She decided she would make them heart-shaped with pink icing. She looked at her wall of cookie cutters. She had different cookie cutters for different occasions. She even had a dog biscuit-shaped one. She found a heart-shaped cookie cutter just the right size. Nikki molded the crispy treats in the heart shape, and by the time the cakes were ready to come out of the oven, the treats were nearly done. Nikki decided to ice the heart shapes when she decorated the next batch of strawberries. She took the three angel food cakes out of the oven and set them aside to cool. Just then, Lidia walked into the kitchen.

"Hey Nikki, there is a young woman here to see you. Do you have a minute? Wow, it smells amazing in here."

"Thanks. I can take a break…did she say who she was?" asked Nikki, washing her hands. Lidia shook her head no. Nikki dried her hands and walked out to the front of the shop, curious.

Lidia trailed after her. "She is sitting at the side table."

Nikki looked and saw a pretty, well-dressed young woman sitting by herself. She was sipping hot chocolate and looking around the store while she waited. Nikki walked over and held out her hand. "Hi, I'm Nikki."

The young woman shook Nikki's hand. "Hi, I'm Becky. I am Susan's maid of honor. Could I talk to you for a minute?" Nikki sighed inwardly but put a smile on her face. Becky was a petite blonde who seemed to be the epitome of calmness and organization. Her heels matched her skirt, and her hair was done up in an impeccable bun.

"Sure. I am between desserts at the moment," Nikki told her while sitting down.

"Your chocolates look amazing," said Becky, glancing at the display cases.

"Thank you. We make all of them ourselves."

"I can tell," said Becky approvingly.

"Is there something I can help you with?" asked Nikki, urging Becky to get to the point.

"Well, I actually stopped by to offer my services. Susan and I have been best friends since kindergarten. I want her wedding to be perfect, and I am willing to do anything to help make that happen, including helping you, if you need me."

"Oh wow, thank you. I appreciate you stopping by, but my crew and I have this under control," replied Nikki. She wondered for a moment if Susan was still worried about the fact that her request for a chocolate table had been last-minute.

"Okay. But if you change your mind and need anything, just let me know," she said, handing Nikki her card. Nikki read it and put it in her apron pocket. "I really want this wedding to be perfect for Susan. She deserves the best. You can call me day or night. I am available for you."

"I understand. I know the whole town is pitching in to make it a dream wedding. I heard the city parks crew is getting double overtime to get the decorations in place," replied Nikki.

"Yes, I think that is wonderful. It is so nice to live in a small town where everyone knows you. And it helps that her dad is the mayor," said Becky with a wink. "Well, I will let you get back to making your chocolates," she said, getting up from the table. "Please do not hesitate to call me if you need anything."

Nikki assured Becky she would call her if she needed her. They got up, and Nikki smiled at her. "It is nice that Susan has such a good friend watching out for her. Please reassure her that everything is right on schedule for the chocolates to be ready for her wedding."

Becky smiled and waved as she left the chocolate shop. Some snow swirled in as the door closed, and Nikki went over to wipe the floor with a dishcloth tucked in her back pocket, making sure it was not too slippery. She stood up and looked out the window. Snow swirled around the park, and people were walking and enjoying themselves. The park was beginning to look magical. She laughed when she saw the mayor trying to reposition a strand of lights around the gazebo. One of the people walking by stopped and gave him a hand. Nikki smiled. It was nice to live in a quaint, small town. Everyone knew each other and was quick to lend a hand when needed. Sure, there were drawbacks, because sometimes you felt like everybody knew your business, but Nikki felt accepted and that was important to her. She wanted to feel safe and to give Seth a safe place to call home. Maple Hills provided that feeling, and it made Nikki both happy and grateful.

She turned and assessed the customers. Tori was helping Nikki's next-door neighbor. Seth was assisting an elderly gentleman, and Lidia was ringing up another customer's order. Lidia looked up and caught her eye over the crowd. She smiled as if to assure Nikki that they had everything under control.

Nikki went back into the kitchen and put away the treats she had made. She washed the dishes and set up a new batch of strawberries for customer orders. Tori and Seth appeared, as the afternoon rush had begun to calm down and it was close to closing time, so Nikki recruited them to help with the strawberries. They stood side by side and cleaned and dipped the strawberries. Nikki liked watching them work together. They were happy, and that made Nikki happy. She was glad to see her son smiling.

Nikki left them to their work and went into the shop. Lidia had a few customers left, and Nikki helped her close up after the customers had left. Nikki put the chocolates away from the display cases, making notes on an inventory sheet as she went along. She remarked to Lidia that they would have to make quite a batch tomorrow to ensure they kept up with customer demand. Lidia nodded as she turned off the hot chocolate machine and started wiping down the counters. After putting away the chocolates, Nikki counted the register and put the deposit in its bank bag. The bank bag always waited under the counter in the evenings. She would have Tori drop it in the night deposit on her way home.

The front door opened, and Nikki looked up to see Hawk walk in. He shook off his coat and stomped his feet, bits of snow falling onto the mat at the front door.

"I knew I should have locked the door sooner," Nikki teased.

"Good evening," he said, bending over to kiss Nikki.

"Your face is cold," she teased and shooed him away.

Hawk laughed. "Hey, how about I cook a big dinner tonight at your place? Everyone can come."

"That sounds perfect," said Nikki. "Would you like to come over?" she asked Lidia.

"Sure. I would love to," Lidia replied. Hawk's cooking was famous and she never missed a chance to enjoy it.

"Let me ask Tori and Seth," said Nikki, walking to the kitchen. She poked her head in and asked them what they were doing that night.

"We don't have any plans," Seth said.

"Well, Hawk is offering to cook, and I hate to pass up that offer," said Nikki with a grin.

"Count us in," said Seth with an enthusiastic whoop. "Does he need any help?"

"I don't think so. Are you almost done with those orders?"

"Yes. We just have one more tray to dip," said Seth.

"Thank you, that is such a big help," said Nikki. "I don't know what I'd do without you guys."

"Oh, Mom. We'd never leave you in the lurch," Seth grinned, wiping his hands on his apron.

Seth and Tori finished the strawberries not long after that, and then drove together and dropped off the deposit. Nikki followed Hawk back to her place. Lidia stopped by her house and then met them all at Nikki's house. Hawk insisted he would cook and that they should all put their feet up. He told Nikki and the crew to relax in the den. Seth went out and retrieved some firewood from the shed and started a warm fire. Nikki sank into the sofa, and Lidia relaxed in the recliner. Seth and Tori sat in the loveseat and talked. They relaxed, watching the flickering flames and chatting happily while Hawk made dinner. As nice as it was to rest her aching feet, Nikki found it hard to sit still when someone else was cooking in her kitchen. After a while she went into the kitchen and offered to help, but Hawk assured her once again he had it under control. From the rich smells of browning meat and savory herbs with caramelized onions filling the kitchen, she had no problem believing him and went back to the den to plan the next day's tasks with Lidia. Soon, Hawk called them to the table; they were greeted with two steaming casserole dishes and a tray of biscuits. Everyone exclaimed how delicious the dinner smelled and thanked Hawk. Hawk was a true genius in the kitchen, the kind of person who could throw something together from just a few ingredients and still feed a crowd and have them begging for more. After dinner, everyone pitched in and washed the dishes. As the night got late, Lidia went home, and Tori left too, yawning. Seth went to his room soon after he finished wiping down the last counter, giving Nikki and Hawk a wave as he disappeared down the hall.

Hawk and Nikki sat on the sofa and relaxed by the fire. It had been a long day, but she was grateful to have such wonderful people around her. Still, she could sense that Hawk was a little tense.

"What are you thinking?" she finally asked him.

"Are you sure you can pull this off?" Hawk asked, worried about Nikki's workload.

"With my family and friends around, I can accomplish anything," she reassured him. "Lidia keeps me on track and reminds me I'm usually ahead of schedule. Seth and Tori always pick up the slack. And then there's you...always swooping in with a delicious dinner just when we think we're all going to collapse on our feet after another busy day." She smiled at him. "It will go just fine." She snuggled under his arm, content to rest quietly in the silence with him. They sat and watched the fire for about half an hour more. Hawk eventually said he needed to go and get some rest. Nikki thanked him and gave him a hug and kiss. She helped him with his coat and opened the door for him. The night sky was full of stars. It was a beautiful crisp evening, with the fresh coating of snow over everything, and Nikki knew she would have no trouble sleeping that night. She waved goodbye to Hawk, locked her door, and went to bed.

chapter three

The next morning, Nikki got up early and had breakfast with Seth. Seth was in an especially good mood because he planned to surprise Tori with tickets to the movies that night. A new romantic comedy had just been released with an actor they both loved to watch, and he thought it would be a nice way to relax at the end of the day. "I'm sure she'll love it, Seth. She knows you adore her and that things have just been busy lately…a nice date will be a good sign, I think." Nikki gave his hand a squeeze as they left the house and he smiled, heartened. When she and Seth drove to the shop, there was already a small group of customers waiting on the sidewalk.

"It is going to be a busy day," Nikki predicted. She was not wrong. As soon as Nikki opened the door, the customers started rolling in. A gentleman asked about the award displayed prominently in the front window. Seth proudly explained that Nikki had won it in a chocolate competition last Christmas. The man was impressed, and Nikki could tell Seth liked to brag about her. She smiled and was once again glad she had entered the competition. Her petit fours had been the talk of the town for two weeks after the competition.

Nikki looked around after she slid another tray of

chocolate hazelnut truffles into the display case. The shop was busy with last-minute Valentine's Day shoppers. Everyone was complimenting Nikki on her chocolate-dipped strawberries. Seth and Tori were helping in the shop while Lidia was working in the kitchen. Tori was helping a young girl pick out a mixed bag of chocolates. The little girl had stopped by Nikki's shop before. She took her time and was careful with her selection. The counters ended up with fingerprints, but Nikki did not mind. The little girl took out her hard-earned allowance to pay for the chocolates and shyly said that she hoped her mother would like the gift. After she left, Nikki wiped off the counters with a smile.

Nikki was in the front waiting on some customers when the door opened and Susan walked in with a handsome gentleman. They were holding hands and each had a twinkle in their eyes. The man could not stop staring at Susan. They were bundled warmly in their coats, with thick sweaters and jeans to keep out the cold. They both looked a bit haggard but happy.

"Nikki," Susan called and waved. She stepped over to the side of the counter while her gentleman removed his jacket and draped it over one of the café chairs.

Nikki waved back. "How are you today?" Nikki asked.

"I'm great. Can we talk for a minute?"

"Sure, just let me finish up here." Nikki finished tying a pretty bow on the chocolate box in front of her. "Here you are, Miss Sims," Nikki said and handed it over the counter to her. Miss Sims smiled and thanked Nikki.

"I recommend this shop to all my neighbors, you know," said Miss Sims as she waved and exited the store. Nikki left the front counter in the capable hands of her son and Tori, fetched three mugs of hot chocolate, and walked over to Susan. Nikki handed them the mugs and sat down.

"Thank you, Nikki. It is cold outside," said Susan. She

took a sip and smiled. "This is delicious. Have you met my fiancé, Tim?"

"I have not," said Nikki.

"It is very nice to meet you," said Tim to Nikki. He was a handsome young man, polite and well-spoken, a perfect match for the lovely young woman.

"You, too. The wedding order is coming along nicely. The chocolates are almost ready, and we have everything we need for the chocolate fountain," Nikki told them.

"Thank you. I am so glad you were able to pull that together. You are amazing. I know the order was last-minute, and I still cannot believe you are pulling it off. Speaking of amazing, I was also hoping you could do me another favor."

"What is that?" asked Nikki, hiding her trepidation.

"The rehearsal dinner is just around the corner, and I was thinking it would be nice to have some chocolates for the guests. You would not have to worry about setting up a table. We will have waiters roaming around with trays," Susan said hopefully. "Only if it's no trouble. I would love to give you some more business for the wedding and...I just thought, perhaps if you have some extra inventory..."

"I am sure I can pull something together. Did you want a certain variety of chocolate, or would you like a sampling of my chocolates?" Nikki asked.

"A sampling sounds terrific, don't you think so, Tim?" Susan asked her fiancé.

"Whatever you want, beautiful," he answered, sipping his cocoa.

"I can get a sampler order done in time for the rehearsal dinner," Nikki assured Susan. "About how many guests will there be?"

"There will probably be around fifty guests that night."

"That will not be a problem at all."

"Thank you so much," Susan exclaimed. "Didn't I tell you she was a lifesaver, Tim?"

"Yes, you did. Thank you, Nikki," Tim said.

"Well, we will let you get to work," Susan said. "Oh, and please come to the rehearsal dinner," she insisted. "And bring a guest."

"Well, I'm not sure. I would not want to intrude. I am happy to make the chocolates, but I thought rehearsal dinners were just for family," Nikki said, hesitating.

"This is less of a rehearsal dinner and more of an informal gathering. We have invited a number of friends from town, and it is a casual affair," Susan said eagerly to Nikki. "I want everyone to be able to compliment you on your fabulous confections, Nikki. You deserve that."

"Okay, I'll be there," agreed Nikki, smiling.

"Wonderful," exclaimed Susan. She and Tim stood up and put their coats on. Tim helped Susan with her coat and scarf. *What a cute couple*, Nikki thought. Tim and Susan left the shop, and Nikki got back to work as a number of customers filled up the shop. After a little while, there was a lull, so Nikki filled in Seth and Tori on the new developments.

"Susan would like a sampling of chocolates for her guests at the rehearsal dinner," Nikki told them. "I told her we would be able to pull it off. I will just need some help." She paused for a moment, worried. Nikki had just remembered that Seth planned to surprise Tori with a date tonight. She met his eyes and tried to give him a reassuring smile.

"I'm sure Lidia can help you sort it out," said Tori.

Seth hugged his mom. "Absolutely," he said.

Just then, the door opened, and Hawk walked in. He brushed the snow off his shoulders and took off his coat. He hung it on the back of a chair and walked over to Nikki, put his arm around her and kissed her hello.

"Just the man I wanted to see," said Nikki.

Hawk raised his eyebrow.

"We have been invited to attend Susan's rehearsal dinner," Nikki said with a smile.

Hawk groaned. "Do I have to wear a suit two nights in a row?" he asked.

"No, silly," Nikki scolded him playfully. "It is casual dressy. You can wear jeans and a nice shirt. No jacket."

"That sounds a little less awful..."

"So, will you join me?" Nikki asked coyly.

"I would be happy to escort you to the dinner," replied Hawk with a half bow. Nikki laughed.

"Why did you stop by?" she asked.

"Actually, I was just passing by and I wanted to drop in and say hello. I'm glad I did, because it sounds like you will need my help."

"I would appreciate that," replied Nikki. She and Hawk went back to the kitchen to let Lidia know what was happening.

"More chocolates?" she exclaimed. "Are you going to be able to handle that?" Lidia was pouring melted chocolate from a large mixing bowl into tiny molds, and there was a smear of pink frosting on her cheek.

"We will be fine," Nikki said with a grin, walking over to dab Lidia's cheek with a kitchen towel. "I have the best crew on the planet."

"Okay, I can stay late if you need me to," said Lidia.

"I appreciate that," replied Nikki.

Seth came in from the front of the store. "Mom, can I talk to you?"

"Sure, Seth," Nikki replied. "What do you need?"

"Nothing...I am just concerned about the amount of work you have taken on for the next couple of days. I know you are strong, but even you have your limits. Tori and I were talking, and we want to help out. I told her about the surprise date I had planned, but she wouldn't hear of it. It won't be any fun for us to go out for a night on the town if we know you're here in the store, working until past midnight. How about we take care of the store orders while you and Lidia work on the wedding and rehearsal chocolates? When we're done with the store orders, we can pitch in with the wedding order."

Nikki was touched at her son's gesture. "Thank you, Seth. That's a very noble offer. Do you agree, Lidia?"

"Yes, I do," Lidia replied, stirring the chocolate with a fond smile. "You're such a wonderful son to your mother, Seth. I know she is proud of you."

"Well, we better get started," Nikki exclaimed. "Many hands make light work, after all." Hawk also offered to help wherever he was needed, explaining that he had the rest of the day off, and she should use him as needed. Nikki smiled as he tied on an apron like a pro.

"Would you mind working in the store?" she asked.

"Sure, if I get busy I will give a yell," Hawk said.

"I will feel safe with you out front," Nikki said sincerely.

"Like I said, I am here to help. Let me run and grab some snacks, first. It looks like it will be another long night."

"That would be a big help. Thank you," Nikki said, putting on her apron. "Okay, where should we begin?" she asked. Seth took one table and Nikki and Lidia took another. Tori watched the shop until Hawk reappeared. He took over and she went back to the kitchen to help the others. Seth prepared the strawberries and Tori dipped and sorted them.

Nikki asked Lidia if they had any extra candies in the freezer. Lidia went to check and came back with a few trays. There were some truffles, chocolate-covered nuts, and chocolate-covered cookies. Nikki had been selling out of her chocolate-dipped strawberries this week, and the other candies, though freshly made, were not selling as fast.

"Those will be perfect for the rehearsal dinner," Nikki said. "I will just make a few more trays of assorted chocolates and we should be set."

"When were you planning on decorating the wedding strawberries?" Lidia asked.

"I will do that tomorrow before the rehearsal dinner," replied Nikki.

"That is cutting it close," said Lidia with concern.

"I should be fine. If I need you to help me, I will let you know."

"Okay," said Lidia. "What do you want me to do right now?"

"Would you make some caramels? We can have some plain caramel, some dipped in chocolate with sea salt, and some with nuts. I can whip up some chocolate, vanilla, and butterscotch fudge. That will set overnight and be ready for tomorrow."

"That sounds like a plan," Lidia replied. The two women got to work on the caramels and fudge, and soon the kitchen filled with the rich smell of melting sugar and butter. Hawk was kept busy in the front of the store and occasionally popped in to ask for help. Seth helped his mother with the trays of assorted chocolates while the fudge was being prepared, and then helped her lay out the massive trays where the fudge would be poured out to cool overnight. The kitchen and the shop were bustling with people and with the delectable smells of wonderful chocolates.

After the store closed, Hawk tidied up front and then came in to help, pitching in with the mountain of dirty pots and baking pans that had accumulated by the sink and the twin dishwashers. Seth, Tori, Lidia, and Hawk stuck at their labors and kept spirits high by singing silly songs and trading jokes, and by ten o'clock, the chocolates were ready for the next day and the kitchen was gleaming. Everyone said goodnight, and Nikki went home to get some much-needed food and sleep.

chapter four

The next morning, Nikki got up before her alarm went off and made some coffee in the pre-dawn chill. She wrote a list of things that needed to get done before the rehearsal dinner that night. She had a sudden realization and ran to check that her outfit was ready. She knew that once she left the house, she would not be back until it was time to get dressed. Everything seemed ready. She opened her closet and picked out a pretty dress in a shade of pale blue that fell just to her knees, with soft brown leather boots. Nikki sorted through her earrings and was looking for the perfect scarf to wear with her dress when she heard Seth in the kitchen making eggs and toast for the two of them.

She walked out of her bedroom with a smile on her face. Her son always remembered to make her a hearty breakfast on days when he knew she would be working like crazy. Nikki sat at the kitchen island and sipped her coffee and ate breakfast with Seth.

"Are you feeling okay?" Seth asked Nikki.

"I'm fine, why?" she asked.

"I just want to make sure you are not overtaxing yourself. You have a habit of taking on more than the average person. You worry so much about others that you forget to worry about yourself. I want you to know that I am here for you." He came around the counter and hugged his mom, and she hugged him back.

"Thank you for having my back," Nikki said and smiled at Seth. "I'm the mom here, I'm supposed to be worrying about you. It's sweet that you worry about me and support me. Are you ready to go?" she asked.

"I will be ready in a minute. Let me clean up in here..." he stood up and she noticed he was still in his flannel pajama pants.

"I will wash the dishes, Seth. You go ahead and get changed."

"Thank you, Mom."

"You're welcome, Seth." Nikki smiled as Seth bounded up the stairs. Even though he was in college, he still bounded around like a Labrador puppy. Nikki smiled fondly as she washed the sinkful of dishes and thought about the day's work ahead. She had most of the chocolates ready for the rehearsal dinner, but she would have to drop them off at the reception hall that afternoon. *I still have to decorate the strawberries*, she remembered. *I can start that this morning. Worst case scenario, I can finish them tomorrow right before the wedding.* Nikki heard a noise and looked up. Seth was coming into the kitchen, humming to himself. Nikki smiled.

"Are you ready to go open the shop?" she asked him.

"Yes. Can I drive?" Seth asked.

"Sure, why not," Nikki replied. She tossed him the keys, and they walked out to the car. Nikki locked the house and then climbed into the car beside Seth. Even though they were from the South, they had grown accustomed to driving in the snow. Seth started down the winding road into town. The trees were dusted with snow, and the fields around Nikki's house looked as smooth as whipped cream. The red feathers of a cardinal caught Nikki's eye, and she watched it hop along the snowy field.

That morning, the shop was just as busy as ever. In the kitchen, Nikki laid out her tools and ingredients to decorate the chocolate-dipped fruit for the wedding. She carefully swirled a flourish of pink chocolate onto each piece that ended in a heart. It was back-breaking work, leaning over the counter and focusing on the berries, and she had to constantly monitor the temperature of the chocolate. After a few hours, Nikki stood up to stretch and was satisfied to see the rows and rows of identical, delicious chocolate-dipped strawberries. She cleaned up the table and turned her mind toward the rehearsal dinner treats. She checked her fudge and the caramels. The trays of fudge had set overnight into a smooth expanse of perfect, solid chocolatey brown, and Lidia's caramels were a tempting shade of golden amber. When she tested the flavor of a caramel, it was the perfect balance of sweetness and buttery flavor. Lidia had cut the caramels into neat, perfect little squares. They looked wonderful. Nikki carefully removed the fudge from its cooling tray and cut it into long pieces, and then into delicate little wedges. She put a few finishing touches on the chocolates, and they were ready to go. Nikki checked the clock. She had become so immersed in the delicious labor of making the chocolates perfect, the day had flown past. It was now almost time to take the candy over to the hall. She quickly arranged the fudge on some trays.

"Hey, Seth," she called.

"Yes?"

"Can you help me load the candies?" Nikki asked.

"As soon as I'm done with this customer," Seth replied.

Nikki started loading the trays into her car. The cold weather would help to keep them fresh and solid. Seth came out with a couple of trays and put them in the trunk.

"Is that all?" he asked.

Nikki counted the trays nervously. "Yes. I have to get my

purse, and I'll be ready to go. I will need you to hold down the fort while I'm gone."

"Aye-aye, captain," Seth said with a mock salute. Nikki grinned, ran and got her purse, and took off for the rehearsal dinner hall.

When Nikki arrived at the rehearsal venue at the appointed drop-off time, she was not sure where to unload her chocolates. She parked in the main lot and went in the front door. There were people running around with last-minute decorations. Nikki stopped one of the decorators and asked where the wedding planner was. The young girl pointed at the bar. Nikki thanked her and walked over. The wedding planner was giving instructions to two waiters in between carrying on a conversation with someone else on the phone. *Impressive multitasking*, Nikki thought. Nikki waited until there was a break in the conversation and then introduced herself.

"Hi, I'm Nikki. Susan asked me to bring some of my chocolates for tonight's dinner."

"Yes, of course," the wedding planner said. "My name is Madeline. You can go ahead and put them in the refrigerators in the back kitchen. If you drive your car around to the back of the building, you can go through the double doors. You will be in a hallway, and the kitchen is the second door on the left."

Nikki thanked her and went back to her car. She drove around and unloaded the chocolates. A couple of waiters were hanging around, and they offered to help her. Nikki thanked them and together they unloaded everything and got it into the refrigerator in a few minutes. Nikki found the wedding planner again.

"The chocolates are in the refrigerator. When will they be served tonight?"

"I plan on serving them after dinner but before our main dessert. Our guests will not have a sit-down meal; instead, the waiters will mingle with trays. Everything is bite-sized, but the quantity will fill everyone up. Your chocolates will make a nice intermission between dinner and dessert."

"That sounds great," Nikki said. "Do you need me to be here early to set up the trays?"

"No, I have an expediter who will be handling that in the kitchen. If you want to check the trays you are welcome to, but he has been doing this for years. He has worked in many five-star restaurants. Only the best for Susan, you know."

"Absolutely," Nikki said. She was impressed with the organization of the evening and felt reassured. Nikki looked at her watch and realized she needed to go home to get ready for the dinner. She thanked Madeline and went to her car. *Maybe I should call Seth and see if the store is busy*, she thought. She called, and there was no answer. *That is odd.* Nikki decided to point the car in the direction of the store.

When Nikki got to the store, she realized why no one had answered the phone. The store was packed. Nikki jumped out of the car and went inside to help. Lidia and Tori were waiting on customers, and Seth was cashiering. Nikki walked behind the counter and started wrapping the chocolates for Lidia and Tori. Both women thanked her. With Nikki's help, the customers were all taken care of quickly. Nikki turned to scold Seth.

"You should have called me," she said.

"It got too busy too quickly," he replied. "Besides, you were delivering the chocolates for the dinner. It all worked out, though."

"Yes, it did. Next time try to call me. I would have gotten here sooner."

"Speaking of time, don't you have to get ready?" Seth asked Nikki.

Nikki looked at her watch. She sighed and smiled at Seth. "Thank you for keeping track of my comings and goings. I do have to run. Please be sure to lock up when you leave for the night."

"I will. Have a great evening," Seth said and hugged his mom around her neck.

"Thank you, I will," she replied. Nikki put on her coat and went out to the car and started driving home. The road was mostly clear, but there were patches of ice. Nikki had to be cautious going up the hill to her house. She was getting better at driving in the snow, but she still erred on the side of caution.

When Nikki got back to her house, she had just enough time to jump in the shower. She blow-dried her hair and put on the clothes she had laid out that morning. Just as she was picking out a pair of earrings to match her blue dress, she heard the front door open.

"Hey Nikki, you in here?" Hawk called.

"I'm upstairs. I will be down in a minute," she said. She finished putting her earrings on and walked down the steps.

Hawk was standing in the foyer. He saw her and whistled. "You look gorgeous," he exclaimed.

"Thank you," Nikki said. "You look quite handsome yourself." She walked over to him, kissed him, and handed him her clutch.

"Hold this, please, while I grab my coat."

"Certainly, but it does not match my shoes," Hawk said. Nikki laughed.

Hawk walked with Nikki to his truck. She slipped on a patch of ice right before she got to the truck and somehow Hawk managed to catch her in his arms.

"Careful now," Hawk chided gently.

Nikki smirked and climbed into the truck. Hawk got in, and they drove to the rehearsal hall together through the early dark of a February evening.

When they walked in, they saw that the hall was decorated beautifully. Nikki realized that what she had seen earlier in the day was barely the beginning of the decorations, and it now looked truly elegant. The waiters were in black and white tuxes, and they were carrying appetizers and drinks around to the guests. There was a band in the corner playing some quiet jazz. The tables had candles and some white and pink flowers arranged in vases. It was simple but elegant. *Just like Susan*, Nikki thought. Hawk saw someone they knew, and they went over to say hello. The rehearsal dinner guests were mingling around, enjoying the food and music.

"Nikki, this is a pleasant surprise," Nikki heard. She turned around and saw the mayor. He was walking toward them with an older gentleman.

"Hello Mr. Mayor and Chief Daily," Nikki said. The chief walked over and gave her a hug. Hawk turned around.

"Hey, Dad," he said to the chief.

"Hey, Hawk," the chief replied. He shook Hawk's hand. "Good to see you here, son."

"I'm looking forward to your chocolates," the mayor said to Nikki with a wink.

"Thank you. I hope you enjoy them," she replied.

"I'm sure they will be delicious," he said. "Knowing you, probably better than that main dessert course the wedding planner picked out."

"If Nikki made them, they will taste like heaven," the chief reassured him.

Nikki blushed and thanked them both for their votes of confidence. She really liked Hawk's father. He was a hard-working man who cared for his son. She had won him over by helping Hawk with some of his cases. When the chief found out her father was a former FBI agent, he had welcomed her with open arms.

A waiter came by with a tray of appetizers. There was a crab claw with deviled crabmeat inside. Nikki thought it was a cute idea and tried one. It was delicious, and the trays looked incredible. Nikki decided she would put her trust in the expediter working in the kitchen to make her chocolates look just as incredible, and just enjoy the night. She and Hawk chatted for some time with the mayor and the chief. The next course came out. It was skewered filet mignon. The steak was cooked a perfect medium rare. Hawk helped himself to two skewers and Nikki laughed.

"Madeline said there would be plenty of food. You don't have to grab it all at once," she joked.

"Who is Madeline?" Hawk asked, devouring a bite from his skewer with a look of bliss on his face.

"She is the wedding planner," Nikki said. "I don't see her on the floor. She is probably in the back driving the waiters crazy," she said. Hawk laughed. Nikki looked around. Everyone was having a good time. She saw Susan and Tim walking around to the different groups. They came over to Nikki's group.

"Thank you for coming, Nikki," Susan said. "And thank you for bringing your chocolates."

"You are welcome." Nikki turned to introduce Hawk.

"Why Hawk, you do dress up well," said Susan. Nikki looked at Hawk.

"Thank you, Susie Q," Hawk said. Susan laughed.

"I haven't heard that nickname in years," she said.

Hawk looked at Nikki. "I have known Susie for many years now. Our fathers have been friends for a long time."

"That makes sense," said Nikki, smiling.

"I see you still haven't lost your appetite," Susan chided

Hawk, looking at his two skewers. "Save enough for everyone."

Hawk laughed. "I will, I promise."

Susan introduced Tim to Hawk, and they shook hands.

"So, you have known Susan for a while?" Tim asked. "You probably have some good stories to share." Susan blushed, and Hawk laughed.

"I think we need to go and say hello to those people over there," Susan said while guiding Tim away from Hawk.

"It was nice meeting you, Hawk."

"You too, Tim." Nikki laughed as Susan led him to the next group.

Soon enough, the waiters had finished serving the trays of the filet mignon skewers and the main course was almost through. She knew they were getting ready to serve her chocolates next. Nikki held her breath. She knew her chocolates were good, but she hoped everyone would like them. She saw the door to the kitchen open and the waiters started walking out with their trays. Nikki gasped.

chapter five

Nikki looked at the trays in amazement. *They are beautiful,* she thought. Each tray had two tiers with an array of small, delicate spoons. On each silver spoon was one of Nikki's chocolates. The glass reflected the light of the room, and the trays glittered while the waiters carried them around. Everyone turned and complimented the presentation with enthusiasm. Everyone in Nikki's group helped themselves to chocolates, and they all praised Nikki on the flavors and designs. Nikki was happy with the displays and was encouraged by the acclamations everyone was throwing her way. She blushed and said thank you a few times.

"See, I told you everyone would love them," said Hawk, giving Nikki's hand a squeeze. Nikki was about to thank him when they heard a clang and the sound of glass breaking. Nikki looked up and saw her chocolates strewn across the floor in a sea of glass. She was livid and embarrassed. Nikki went over to the back corner of the room to give the waiter a piece of her mind, but then she noticed he looked like he was in shock. She stopped and looked where he was staring. Someone was slumped over at the corner table. Nikki recognized her as one of Susan's bridesmaids, whom she'd met earlier that evening.

She ran over to the table, her footsteps crunching over the glass. Hawk called after her and then followed to see what the commotion was about. The waiter was feeling for the girl's pulse. He looked pale. The woman looked even worse.

"I just thought she was drunk," the waiter told Nikki. Nikki turned and saw Hawk. She shook her head back and forth. Hawk moved the waiter to the side and checked for a pulse. There was none. Hawk quickly got on the phone, and Nikki could hear him calling the precinct. She heard him explain what had happened and affirm that he was taking control of the scene. Nikki told the waiter to have a seat at a nearby table. When Nikki turned around, she saw a wave of people approaching with Susan and Tim at the crest. Nikki physically stopped them and told Tim to take Susan across the room and have her sit down.

"That's Kim," Susan exclaimed while Tim held her back. "Is she okay?"

"Please get her out of here," Nikki pleaded. Tim held Susan close and guided her to the other side of the room. He sat her at a table and asked a waiter to bring them some water.

Nikki asked the other guests to have a seat. She let them know that the police were on the way and that they all needed to stay in the building. The chief appeared, and Nikki explained to him what was happening. He thanked her for calming the crowd down and told her he could take it from there. Nikki decided to see how Susan was doing. She walked over to the table where Susan was sitting with Tim.

"I am so sorry, Susan," Nikki started. "I know this is shocking for you, but I need you to try to stay as calm and as focused as you can." Susan nodded, but she had a vacant look in her eyes.

"We are not sure what has happened yet, but Kim is dead," Nikki told her. She hated having to tell people their friends and relatives had died. She admired Hawk more every time she had to relay this news. Nikki only had to do this occasionally, but for Hawk, it was part of his job.

"The police will be here soon," she continued, holding on to Susan's hand. Tim had his arm around her. Susan was looking pale. Nikki was afraid she might faint. "Do you have her parents' number so we can notify them?"

"Could you get me a bag of ice?" Nikki asked a nearby waiter. He left and returned with a small bag. "That is fine," Nikki said. She instructed Tim to hold this on the back of Susan's neck.

"I can't just sit here," Tim said angrily. "What happened to Kim? She was fine an hour ago. Who is in charge?" Tim started to get up, but Nikki took him by the hand.

"Please. Susan needs you right now. Hawk and Chief Daily are in charge of the investigation. I know they will fill you in as soon as they have any answers," Nikki reassured him. Tim sat back down and held Susan. Nikki noticed the crowd getting a little louder. She got up and found Chief Daily.

"I think people may be starting to panic," she told the chief.

"I think you're right," he said. The chief raised his voice and asked for silence. There was the sound of muffled weeping, but everyone's attention was on the chief.

"I know this has been a rough evening. I ask you for your continued patience. We will need to interview everyone here before you leave. I will set up an interview table in the back hallway. Nikki will come and get you when I want to speak with you. Everyone just remain calm, and we will get through this in an orderly fashion. Once I have talked with you, you will be cleared to go home."

The guests seemed to calm down. Nikki was going to ask the chief who he wanted to talk with first when she saw

Becky, Susan's maid of honor. She was crying, so Nikki went over to talk to her. Nikki gave Becky a hug.

"I know this must be hard. Can I ask you for a favor, though?" Becky looked at Nikki, sniffed, and nodded.

"Could you please keep an eye on Tim and Susan? She really needs you by her side right now."

Becky nodded again, wiping away her tears and looking a little heartened to have a task to do, and Nikki left the three of them at the table together. Nikki talked to the chief, and they decided to talk to the bridal party first, then the families, other guests, and staff. While the chief was questioning the witnesses, Hawk was talking with the local police. Nikki did not have a chance to go near him, as the chief had her hopping. Nikki did notice when the medical examiner arrived and the body was bagged. They took Kim to the morgue for an autopsy. It was a long night with a lot of paperwork to get through – so many statements. Finally, the last guest was questioned, cleared, and sent home. Hawk and the chief talked for a few minutes, and then Hawk came over to where Nikki was sitting, sipping some water a waiter had brought her.

"Are you ready to go home?" Hawk asked.

"Absolutely," Nikki said, exhausted. Hawk helped her up, and they went to his truck. He drove her home and followed her into the house. Seth and Tori were there. They looked anxious.

"We heard what happened," Seth said. "Are you okay?"

"Yeah," said Nikki, giving Seth a hug. "I'm sorry to have worried you, I should have called earlier, but we were so busy. I'm just stopping by the house to get changed. Hawk and I are going to head to the station."

Seth started to interrupt her, "But Mom, you look exhausted..."

"I will be fine," Nikki reassured him.

"I tried calling you, and you didn't answer," he said.

"I'm sorry. I was caught up in the middle of everything. I will try to remember to check my phone next time."

"Okay. I'm just glad you are both okay," he reiterated. Tori squeezed Seth's hand in solidarity and they sat on the couch, talking in low tones about the events of that night.

Nikki went up to her bedroom. The bed was calling to her, but she knew Hawk would need help with this case. She had helped him before, and he had appreciated it. She was not only a witness, she was an experienced investigator by this point, and she was needed by the man that she loved. She changed into jeans and a warm, blue cable-knit sweater and went back downstairs.

"You know, if you need to rest, I can take care of this," Hawk said.

"I will be fine," said Nikki, feeling the rush of adrenaline she always got when working on a case. Nikki knew this would keep her awake, so she might as well be awake by Hawk's side.

"Okay," Hawk answered. His fierce hug told her that he appreciated her fortitude in the face of such a perplexing case.

"Let's have a cup of coffee before we go," suggested Nikki.

"I already have a pot brewed," answered Tori, appearing with four cups. Nikki thanked her, and they sat at the table and drank their coffee.

"How was business today?" Nikki asked.

"We had quite a few customers after you left," said Tori. "Seth was a big help, of course."

"Good. I am so glad you are home on break," Nikki said to Seth.

"Perfect timing," he replied with a smile.

"Okay, we had better get to the station before I get too comfortable," Hawk said, passing a hand over his eyes. He and Nikki put on their coats and said goodbye to Seth and Tori, heading back out into the icy winter night.

When they got to the station, Hawk headed right for the chief's office. He looked up wearily and told them to sit down. He gave Nikki a weary but grateful smile. Hawk asked what the chief had learned from questioning the guests.

"Well, most of them had not noticed Kim except when the wedding party came over to talk to them. Becky and Susan told me that Kim was acting strange, but they thought she had just had one too many cocktails. She was weaving around and slurring her words, saying she was tired. Her friends sat her at the table with a glass of water, hoping she'd sober up enough to enjoy the dessert course with everybody. Her friends went back to mingling with the party, and they were just as shocked as everyone else when she was found dead. I will be talking to them again tomorrow morning."

"Was the cause of death alcohol poisoning?" asked Nikki.

"We're not sure. The cause of death is still to be determined. We do not think it was alcohol poisoning, but it was some kind of poisoning. Her lips and fingernails were blue. Other things can cause a person to appear drunk. I am going to run some samples to the lab right now and put a rush order on things." He tapped the open box on his desk that contained a number of glass vials of tissue and serum samples.

"Can you call us when you get the toxicology report?" Hawk asked him.

"Absolutely," the chief replied, standing up with the box of vials, ready to leave.

"What do you want us to do right now, Chief?" Hawk pressed.

Chief Daily paused and looked at him and Nikki. "Son, we have so many statements to review…there's no sense in you two trying to stay up overnight. You'd never get through it all. I'd much rather you got a good night's sleep so you can be fresh for tomorrow." Hawk nodded at his father's words.

They all stood and put on their coats. Hawk and Nikki followed the chief down the hall and out to the parking lot.

"Drive safely, Dad," Hawk said to the chief. They shook hands, and the chief got in his car and pulled out of the parking lot.

Hawk turned to Nikki. "I'll give you a ride home."

"Thank you. Why don't you stay on my sofa tonight?" Nikki suggested. "Who knows when the chief will call, and this way you and I can come back together." Despite her love for Hawk, she was still old-fashioned about some things in a relationship, and so was Hawk. The sofa was the best option.

"That sounds like a good idea," answered Hawk. He opened the car door for Nikki. They got in and he pointed the car towards her house. When they got to the house, Seth was still waiting up, but said goodnight with a yawn and left for bed. Hawk made up the sofa and said goodnight to Nikki. Nikki went to her room, her feet dragging on the stairs. *I hope I can get some sleep tonight,* she thought. She turned off her light and closed her eyes.

chapter six

Nikki was sleeping soundly when she felt a hand on her shoulder. Someone was shaking her gently. She opened her eyes and saw Hawk standing over her.

"What time is it?" Nikki asked.

"It is around 4 a.m.," Hawk told her. "The chief called. The toxicology report is in."

Nikki woke up quickly. "What were the results?"

"It looks like a heroin overdose," Hawk told her.

The shock woke Nikki completely. "A heroin overdose?" she asked, sitting up.

"Yes," Hawk said.

"Had Kim ever done heroin before?" Nikki asked.

"I did not think so," Hawk replied, "but you would be surprised at the number of people who use drugs and no one ever knows. It seems we have a new line of questioning to investigate with her friends."

"Let me get dressed and we can go in," Nikki told Hawk. He left, and she threw on some jeans, a sweater, and boots. Nikki rushed down the stairs where Hawk was waiting with her coat. She left a note for Seth on the kitchen table and shrugged on her coat, adrenaline racing through her once again. It was so early that as Hawk drove them to the station they encountered no traffic. It was still dark, and the moonlight lit up the snow, turning it bluish in color. Nikki watched the snow out her side of the truck and it was a grim reminder of Kim's face and hands.

Hawk rushed to the station, and they went inside. The officer at the front desk told Hawk his father was talking to the medical examiner. Hawk and Nikki went down the hallway to the medical examiner's office and went in. He and the chief were talking in the corner. They stopped when they saw Hawk and Nikki.

"Come on in," the medical examiner said to Hawk and Nikki.

"What have you found out?" asked Nikki.

"Well, there does not appear to be any evidence of prior heroin use," said the examiner. "There are no track marks present on her arms, no injection wounds on her arms or feet. She appeared healthy, except for the large amount of heroin in her system. I did, however, find a puncture mark in her neck."

"That is odd," said Nikki.

"That's what I thought," said the chief.

The medical examiner took them over to the body. He showed them her clear arms and feet. He showed them the puncture mark in her neck. It was small. Nikki was impressed that the medical examiner had found it.

He explained further that he would send some of Kim's hair to be tested for prior heroin use, just in case. Strands of hair could show opiate use from a month ago, or longer. "Based on the lack of injection sites, however, I'm doubtful about that. Her medical history doesn't show any prescribed opiates, either. My theory," said the medical examiner, "is that someone injected this young lady with pure heroin. They injected it into her neck, and it caused her to overdose."

"That's so awful," said Nikki, feeling sick to her stomach.

"It would explain why her friends thought she was

drunk," said Hawk. "A heroin overdose is similar to alcohol poisoning. It can cause some similar symptoms, like sleepiness, slurred speech. I can understand why her friends thought she was drunk." The medical examiner covered up the body.

Nikki nodded. "We should go talk with Susan, Becky, and the rest of the wedding party," she suggested. Hawk agreed. The chief said he would send deputies to pick up a few of Kim's friends and bring them in for questioning. Hawk and Nikki volunteered to go to the hotel where the wedding party was staying. Nikki remembered that Susan had told her they were staying in the hotel so they could be together the night before her wedding. "She told me that at the party," she told Hawk and the chief.

"If we go there, we can question them quickly and figure out if anyone else has a history of drug use," Hawk said. The chief agreed. Hawk and Nikki quickly left in Hawk's truck and drove to the hotel.

When they got there, the front desk was abandoned. Hawk rang a bell on the desk, and a sleepy manager appeared after a few minutes. Hawk showed the man his badge and asked what rooms the wedding guests were staying in, specifically the bride, groom, and their attendants. The man gave Hawk the room numbers. Hawk requested to use the conference room, and the man agreed. He also asked the manager to brew some coffee and have it ready in the conference room. It was going to be a long morning.

Hawk and Nikki split up. Nikki went to Susan's room, which was near all her bridesmaids, and Hawk went to Tim's room, near the groomsmen and best man's rooms. They woke up the guests and asked them to go to the conference room for more questioning. Susan was upset, and Nikki reassured her that everything was going to be okay. She explained that she and Hawk just needed a little more information. Susan agreed, and Nikki ushered her and her gaggle of sleepy, tearful girls down to the conference room. Tim was already there, and Susan rushed over to him. They hugged and sat together at a table.

Hawk and the manager talked, and the manager set up a room for Hawk to question the guests. Although usually they would separate people before questioning so they could not coordinate their stories, Hawk had suggested that the group atmosphere might relax everyone's nerves and help convey the message that no one was a suspect yet. This was true. But Nikki desperately hoped they would find a clue that would lead them somewhere today. She suggested they talk to Susan and Tim first so they could get back to sleep.

"It is her wedding day, after all," said Nikki. Hawk agreed. When it was clear that Susan was still shaky and tearful about her friend's death, they also agreed to question them together. Nikki called Susan and Tim back to the smaller room set up by the manager.

"I am so sorry to be doing this right now," said Hawk to the couple.

"That's okay," said Tim. "We are willing to do anything you need, right sweetie?" he asked Susan.

"That's right," said Susan, putting on a brave face despite her tears.

Hawk proceeded to question Susan and Tim. They both had alibis for the day, which was expected. A bride and groom on the day before their wedding were never alone, what with final fittings at the tailors for the men, and hair and makeup consultations for the ladies, and a dozen other errands. The couple had always been with someone, and the questioning went quickly. Neither had seen anything to indicate that their dear friend had struggled with any addictions, either. Hawk finally thanked them and told them they could go back to their rooms. With obvious relief, Susan and Tim thanked him and quickly left.

Next Nikki asked Becky to come in. She entered, and they

talked for a few minutes. She, too, had an alibi for the day. She was either with Susan all day or one of the bridesmaids or Susan's mother all day long. They told her she could return to her room. After that, they questioned the rest of the bridal party one by one. They were all cleared and told to go back to their rooms. Afterward, Hawk and Nikki called the chief.

"Everyone in the party has been vetted," said Hawk. The chief said he had questioned Kim's friends as well, and he had no suspicions of any of them.

"Maybe we should talk to the wedding planner and the wait staff again," suggested Nikki.

"That is a good idea," said Hawk. He told his father they were headed to the venue. Nikki was certain the wedding planner would be there. By then, it was seven in the morning and light was beginning to spread across the little town, but it was still frosty and cold.

As they approached the building, Nikki told Hawk to park in the back by the service entrance. Sure enough, there were cars in the parking lot. Nikki and Hawk entered and found the staff setting up for the wedding reception. Nikki asked a young man carrying chairs where to find Madeline.

"She is in the foyer. I think she is overseeing the guest cards," the staff member replied. Nikki and Hawk went to the front of the building and found Madeline instructing an assistant on how to arrange the cards on the table. Nikki and Hawk walked up to her and Hawk cleared his throat. Madeline turned around and told the young woman to continue what she was doing, and she would come by to check it later.

"What can I do for you?" she asked Nikki and Hawk. "Are you here to set up your table?" she asked Nikki. Nikki panicked for a moment. She had forgotten the table she was supposed to set up. She took a deep breath and told herself to calm down. She could get through this. Meanwhile, Hawk cut in to inform Madeline that they needed to question the staff.

"Again?" asked Madeline a bit sharply. "I am on a tight schedule here. I do not have time to be answering questions."

"I understand that you are busy," replied Hawk. "I promise this should not take long. We will interview people one at a time. Nikki can arrange everything and make sure we do not miss anyone. They can keep working before and after we question them."

"Okay," Madeline said, though she did not sound reassured. She knew there was no use arguing with the detective. "Who do you want to talk to first?" she asked.

"Why don't we start with you?" Hawk answered.

"Of course," Madeline said smoothly. "Fire away."

"Can you give me a list of workers?" Nikki asked Madeline. "That way I can get people organized while Hawk is questioning you."

"Okay. It is here in this folder," Madeline answered Nikki, handing her a manila folder. Nikki thanked her and started reading down the list. Hawk took Madeline into a small room and shut the door. Nikki walked around and checked to make sure everyone was there and gathered phone numbers and addresses to save time during the questioning. Nikki explained that Hawk had some follow-up questions and that they would be called in alphabetical order. A few of the staff members looked at each other, and Nikki wondered if some of them had been traumatized by the events last night. They went on working and waited to be called.

When Hawk sent Madeline out after questioning, Nikki told her how she would be calling the staff. Madeline agreed and went back to the foyer to continue supervising the guest cards while Nikki ushered the next person in. Luckily, the whole process went just as smoothly as it had with the wedding party. Nikki wondered what Hawk was going to find, however. When he was done with everyone, they found Madeline and thanked her.

"So, why are you still questioning people?" she asked. "I

thought I heard people say she died of alcohol poisoning. It's so sad, she's so young."

"I am not at liberty to discuss the case right now," said Hawk. "I will ask that you and your staff be ready for more questions as needed. We have your contact information."

Madeline sighed and agreed. She went back to work and Hawk and Nikki returned to the parking lot.

"Everyone is clear," said Hawk once they were outside. "No one stands out as a suspect."

Just then, Hawk's phone rang. "It's the chief," he told Nikki. He talked to him for a few minutes and then hung up.

"What did he say?" asked Nikki.

"Dad said the mayor is hopping mad. He refuses to cancel the wedding and wants to know what is happening with the investigation. Dad did not want to tell him anything at first, but the mayor threatened to fire him. Dad figures he's just upset, but he doesn't want to risk his job. He told the mayor about the overdose. He said the mayor was shocked. He's known his daughter's friend for years and said Kim did not seem the type to use drugs. He badgered him for more details until he revealed that they suspected foul play." Hawk paused a moment. "See, this is why my father is such a good police chief. He knows the mayor will never come in for questioning, but he might reveal a few details if he thinks he's getting inside information." Hawk smiled.

"So what did the mayor say?" Nikki was tense.

"The mayor went quiet for a couple of seconds. He said that Susan had appeared worried when he had talked to her last night, after it all happened. The mayor said she told him that Susan and Tim were worried that someone was out to get them. Of course, the chief asked him why Susan and Tim would think that. The mayor told him Susan said she just had a gut feeling. Susan still did not know about the overdose at that time, of course. The chief told him that he did not suspect Susan and Tim's lives were in danger, but he could not rule it out. Well, that did it. The mayor is now demanding that the investigation be wrapped up quickly. He wants a suspect found before the wedding. The mayor authorized overtime and told us to mobilize as much manpower as we need. After all, Susan is his little girl and this will be her special day, by hook or by crook." Hawk grimaced.

"Well, I guess we've got our work cut out for us. Let's head back into town," suggested Nikki.

"Okay," agreed Hawk. "You can help me review the witness statements."

"I wish I could Hawk, but maybe later…I still need to finish up the chocolates for the wedding," Nikki said.

Hawk agreed to take her to the shop, and they drove into town. As they drove, Nikki looked at her phone. Seth had sent a message saying Tori had picked him up and driven him to the shop. They were already there with Lidia. He told Nikki not to worry, they had the shop covered. *Yeah, but who has the wedding covered?* she thought as they neared town.

chapter seven

Nikki was feverishly at work decorating a tray of chocolates when Hawk came in. He had gone to his office to check in and consolidate his notes. Nikki was finishing the icing on the strawberries. They all looked beautiful. Seth and Tori were helping her with the chocolates. They were putting some finishing touches on the other fruit. Hawk came into the kitchen, followed by Lidia, and said hello.

"How are the chocolates coming? You ready to get back to the investigation? We still have plenty of time before the wedding later today," he said.

Nikki twirled the icing bag with a flourish and pulled it up. "Done," she said. "All I have to do is cut the angel food cake, and we are ready to go." She glanced desperately at the clock. "Oh no, is that the time? We're supposed to deliver the chocolates right now!"

"I can cut the cake," Lidia offered.

"Yes, and we can take everything to the venue," Seth chimed in.

"If they take the chocolates and come right back, I can run the store by myself for at least an hour if need be," said Lidia.

"This is our busiest day of the year," argued Nikki, despairing.

"Yes, but most of our customers have placed and picked up their orders already. I can handle the last-minute traffic, and it will not take Seth and Tori long to set up the table. They will be back before I know they are gone," Lidia reassured Nikki.

"Well, okay," Nikki agreed.

"Good," said Hawk. "I'll drive you home and meanwhile we can catch up about the investigation. I have been going over my notes and have not gotten any further. Maybe if we go over everything again together, we will think of another angle to investigate."

"Okay," said Nikki. "Just let me clean up and get this apron off."

She washed her hands and hugged Seth, Tori, and Lidia. "Thank you for being such a great team," she said.

"The team is only as good as its leader," remarked Lidia. Nikki smiled as she and Hawk left the shop.

The town green was starting to become crowded with wedding guests and decorators. The center of town was transforming into a swirl of red and white. The tents and awnings were up and the chairs and tables were being arranged for the wedding. A man walked by carrying two tables, and Hawk and Nikki jumped out of his way.

"Shall we head right for your place?" suggested Hawk.

"Okay, we can have some coffee and talk about the case," said Nikki. They headed for his truck.

"That sounds good." Hawk opened the passenger door for Nikki, and she stepped into his truck. She yawned.

"Yes, we will definitely need some caffeine," she said. Hawk laughed and they started for Nikki's house. When they got to the house, Nikki brewed some coffee, extra strong. She looked in the freezer and found the extra batch of brownies she had made the week before.

"These should still be good."

"I'll take two," Hawk insisted. She popped a few in the microwave to warm them up, craving a little sugar herself. Nikki plated them and poured the coffee. *Caffeine and chocolate will get us through anything,* she thought. Hawk opened his file and put his notes on the table. Nikki and Hawk sat in the kitchen and sipped their coffee perusing the notes. There did not seem to be anything they had missed.

"So, we cleared the staff at the venue," Nikki began.

"Yes," said Hawk.

"And we cleared the bridal party."

"Yes."

"And we cleared the guests."

"Yes, yes, and yes," replied Hawk, stretching. Hawk seemed a bit snippy, but Nikki knew it was because he was so fatigued and so concerned about the case. His father had to wrap this up quickly and with no leads, it looked like it would not be possible. They were both worn down after a night of barely four hours of sleep, but were determined to figure out what happened to Kim. Nikki poured Hawk some more coffee. She poured herself half a mug more. She did not want to get jittery from the sugar and caffeine rush.

"Maybe we should talk to Susan again," Nikki suggested.

"I'm not sure about that," said Hawk. "It is her wedding day. Her father would have a fit if he saw us bothering her." Nikki agreed, and she did not want the chief to have to deal with the mayor again. However, they had no leads, and talking to Susan again might help. She had been Kim's closest friend.

"That's true, but if I went alone, I bet I could talk to her," said Nikki. "She should be at her parents' house getting ready. I heard she was taking bridal party pictures there before the wedding. I don't mind going there and talking to her."

"Okay," said Hawk, "but if the mayor appears..."

"I will smile and start talking about chocolates," finished Nikki. Hawk smiled.

On the ride to the mayor's house, Nikki thought of how to approach Susan. She decided to feel out the situation and go from there. Nikki pulled up to the house and parked. The house was a two-story mansion in town. It had a circular driveway, and Nikki half expected to see a valet. Nikki walked to the front door and found it was open. Nikki walked in and saw someone who looked like a photographer's assistant rushing past. "Excuse me, can you tell me where Susan is?" The woman pointed to the dining room. There were people running around, and the mayor's wife was barking orders at everyone as they prepared for the photo shoot. Someone was carrying flowers and others carried trays of food. There was a person beside the mayor's wife on a cell phone. She seemed to be the mayor's wife's personal assistant. In the middle of this storm, Susan was sitting at the dining room table sipping some tea. She looked happy but tired. *Overwhelmed, just like any bride on her wedding day,* thought Nikki. Susan perked up and gave her a happy wave. Nikki slid in and sat down next to Susan.

"How are you holding up?" she asked Susan.

"As well as can be expected," Susan replied. "Would you like some tea?"

"No thank you. I was wondering if I could ask you a couple of questions."

"Sure, but let's go up to my room. It is too busy down here." Susan got up, and her mother demanded to know where she was going. Susan explained that she just needed a little girl talk with Nikki in her room. Her mother opened her mouth to object, but Susan cut her off.

"Mom, I just need a few minutes of quiet," she said. Her

mom made an exasperated face, but waved her away, turning to start barking orders at someone else.

Nikki followed Susan up the stairs to her room. The stairs were wide and curved to the top with an elegant balustrade of wrought iron and carved wood. Susan's bedroom was a suite with a sitting room and bedroom. There was a set of sliding doors that led to a balcony. Susan shut the door and sat on her bed. She motioned to Nikki to sit on a loveseat nearby. Nikki looked around at the flowered wallpaper and the chic miniature chandelier hanging above the fireplace. It was a gorgeous room befitting the mayor's daughter.

"It must be so strange to be having this special day without your friend. I'm sure you thought about postponing the wedding, right?" Nikki prodded.

"No. This has been planned for quite some time. I am still getting over Kim's death, but all our loved ones are already here, everything is prepared...I want to get married to Tim today." Susan pulled out some tissues and wiped her eyes. She was keeping herself together – but barely.

"I understand. I was concerned because your father mentioned you and Tim thought someone was out to get you."

Susan looked up as if she was a little surprised that Nikki knew this detail. "Well, since someone killed one of my bridesmaids at my wedding party, can you blame me?" Susan asked.

"That makes sense," Nikki replied. Nikki wanted to console her, but she knew she had to ask the hard questions. That was the only way she and Hawk would solve this case. "Do you know anyone who would want to hurt you or Tim?"

"No, that is why I am so scared. We do not have any enemies. This is totally out of the blue," Susan replied. Nikki could feel Susan getting anxious. "I mean, it happened at my rehearsal dinner. Was someone after us?"

"That's what we are trying to find out," Nikki reassured her. "Do you know if Kim had any enemies?"

"No. She was a sweet, loving person," Susan replied.

"Had she been acting weird?"

"No. Not that I know of. Like I told you at the hotel – she's a close friend, but we are not together all the time. I suppose there are others who might know more than me. You questioned her roommate already, I assume?" Susan said.

"Was she at the rehearsal dinner last night? The roommate, I mean."

"No, it's a he. He is, was, just her roommate," Susan replied, catching herself using the wrong tense. "His name is John Hammer." She gave Nikki his information and Nikki wrote it down. She felt a surge of adrenaline again as she recognized this as a significant lead. She knew that the friends of Kim's who were questioned were all female, which meant no one had talked to John Hammer yet.

"Is that all?" asked Susan. "I'm glad you came by...but I don't have much time to sit and talk. My makeup artist is due here any moment and I'm booked all day leading up to the wedding."

"Of course. Absolutely," Nikki said. "I appreciate you taking the time." Just then, there was a knock on the door.

"Susan, are you in there?" a woman asked.

"Yes, Mom. I will be back down in a minute."

"We are on a tight schedule, you know. And Jillian is here."

"Okay," Susan replied, rolling her eyes. "That's my makeup appointment." Nikki smiled.

"Well, thank you. I will be going now. If you think of anything else, please give me a call."

"I will," promised Susan. Nikki left the room and swiftly went down the stairs. She made it out the door without running into the mayor. She got to her car and called Hawk.

"Kim had a roommate," she told him. "A male roommate."

"That is new," Hawk replied. "What's the roommate's name?"

"His name is John Hammer, and they lived on the other side of town. I'll text you his address. Meet me there," Nikki replied. Hawk agreed. Nikki got in the car and decided to call Seth to see how things were going.

"Is everything coming together?" she asked.

"Yes, we are getting all the ingredients for the chocolate fountain ready and all the trays of chocolates lined up."

"Good," Nikki said.

"How is the investigation coming?" Seth asked.

"We have some new information that might help, but it's too soon to tell."

"That's good. You know, I met Kim a while ago. We have a friend in common," Seth said. Nikki was surprised.

"Why didn't you tell me that?" she asked.

"I guess it slipped my mind until now."

"Will you do me a favor?"

"Yes," Seth said.

"Can you find out if Kim was dating her roommate? His name is John."

"Okay. I will call my friend and get back to you."

"Thank you," Nikki replied. She hung up the phone and drove to the address Susan had given her. *I wonder what John Hammer will be like*, she thought as the trees rushed by her car. Nikki thought about the wedding, but then pushed that out of her mind. *Seth and the others are taking care of things*, she thought. *Everything will be fine.* She turned on the radio and hummed along with an old country song.

chapter eight

Nikki drove to Kim's apartment. It was a cute duplex in a small, quiet neighborhood. There were flowerpots on the porch and a swing. The flowerpots were empty and covered in a thin layer of snow. The lawn was small but well kept. The hedges around the house were covered and looked as soft as marshmallows. She looked around and saw that the neighboring houses were close, but not on top of one another. Nikki parked and waited for Hawk. She did not have to wait very long.

Hawk pulled up in front of Nikki and got out of his truck. Nikki got out and together they walked to the front door. Hawk knocked, and Nikki stood behind him. The front door opened and a man appeared behind the screen door. He was nice-looking, with short blond hair. He was shorter than Hawk but taller than Nikki. He was clean shaven. Nikki guessed that he was older than Kim but not by very much. The man was visibly upset, his eyes were a little reddened and there was a sad slump to his otherwise handsome physique. Hawk introduced himself and Nikki while showing the man his badge.

"I am Hawk Daily. I'm a detective with the Maple Hills police department. This is my partner, Nikki Bates. She assists me with some of my investigations. Are you John Hammer?" he asked the man.

"Yes, I am. Is this about Kim?"

"Yes. We are here to ask you some questions about her. Would you mind if we came in?"

"Sure, come on in. I am willing to answer any questions you may have." He held the screen door open, and Hawk and Nikki stepped inside and were in the duplex's living room. Nikki noticed a small bookshelf by the door to the right, and a sofa and entertainment center. Straight ahead was a dining room. There were knick-knacks and pictures of Kim on top of the bookshelf. John offered them the sofa, and he sat down in a recliner facing them. He asked if they wanted any coffee. Hawk thanked him but declined.

"Let's get right to the questions, okay?" Hawk said. "Were you and Kim dating?"

"Yes," said John. Nikki was shocked but did not show it.

"How long were you dating?" Hawk asked.

"We have been together for three years."

"If you were dating, why weren't you at the rehearsal dinner?" Nikki asked.

"Susan does not approve of me," he said, looking down.

"What do you mean by that?" asked Hawk.

"She and I have never gotten along. When Kim introduced us and Susan asked what I did for a living, I told her and she got very judgmental. She thinks I am a bad influence on Kim."

Nikki gazed around the apartment. It was small, but nicely furnished. There were flowers on the coffee table and some magazines. It was cozy and inviting. She did not get a bad vibe from the place. "Why does she think you're a bad influence?" she asked John.

"She thinks I'm a bad influence because of what I do and where I work," he said. John shifted in his seat. "I am a rehabilitation psychologist. I counsel former drug addicts.

Some of my clients are former drug dealers. They are not people Susan would approve of."

Hawk and Nikki looked at each other. "Do any of your clients know where you live?" asked Hawk.

"No. I keep my work and private life separate. What I do is a good thing that could be exploited by bad people. Some of the people I work with do get rehabilitated. They go on to become productive members of society. Others, well, they do not turn out as well and sometimes end up back in jail. I do not want them to find me in case they blame me for landing back in prison. I would never put Kim in that kind of danger."

"How do you keep your work and personal life separate?" Hawk asked.

"I have taken quite a few precautions. It's part of the work. I use a partial alias, John Jackson instead of John Hammer – Jackson is my middle name, you see. We keep a post office box so that we don't have to give out our address except to close friends. My office is an hour away. I take different routes to work each day, and I make sure I am not followed. My car is a rental in my alias. If someone wanted to find me by tracing the license plate, they would have a very hard time. I have always strived to keep myself and those I care about safe. Kim meant the world to me, and I would never do anything to put her in danger." John stared at the floor and tears welled in his eyes. He wiped his eyes and looked up when Hawk spoke.

"Are you aware of the circumstances surrounding Kim's death?" Hawk asked.

"No," John gulped.

"She died of a heroin overdose."

John turned pale. He shook his head violently. "She would never do that. Kim was a sweet and special woman. She was strong. She had no reason to use heroin, let alone overdose. I would know if she was using drugs. I have been trained to spot addicts, especially opiate users."

"We believe you," said Nikki gently. John wiped his eyes. He looked out the window and tears started to fall again. He was visibly shaken. Nikki looked at Hawk.

"Do you know anyone who would want to hurt Kim? Was she arguing with anyone? Did anyone hold a grudge against her for any reason?" Nikki asked.

"No, absolutely not. Kim was kind. She was gentle. She would feed the stray cats in the neighborhood. She once let a neighbor's child stay here while the neighbor was stuck in another town with car trouble. Everyone loved her and knew they could count on her. I work with some very hardened people. Kim was the opposite of that. She was open, honest, and beautiful."

"If you don't mind, we would like you to come down to the station for further questioning," Hawk said quietly but firmly.

"Yes. Absolutely," John said. He wiped his eyes. "I can follow you down there right now. I will do whatever it takes to find out what happened to Kim. Let me get changed first. I have not been out of these clothes since last night." John went up the stairs to his bedroom. Nikki turned to Hawk when he was out of earshot.

"That is an odd way of doing business," she said.

"Well, it can be a dangerous line of work," Hawk said. "Drug addicts can be unpredictable and violent at times, people in recovery can relapse. I think it is a good idea that he uses an alias. He wanted to keep himself and Kim safe. I understand that need."

Nikki looked at him. "I understand, too," she said. They sat for a short time and then John came back down the stairs.

"Are you ready to go?" Hawk asked him.

"Yes, I have my wallet and keys. My car is parked on the street."

"We are parked there, too," Nikki said.

They all put on their coats. Nikki and Hawk walked down the sidewalk side by side. Nikki said she would go to the station, too. Hawk asked if she needed to check in with Seth.

"No. I called him before we came over here. He should be calling me back, soon," she said.

"Okay. Let's go right to the station then," Hawk suggested. "Are you sure you don't want a ride?" he asked John.

"No, I will follow you. I think driving alone in the car will help me get my mind straight. I could use the fresh air. I have not been outside since yesterday," he admitted.

"Okay," said Hawk. They got in their separate cars and drove down to the station. Nikki followed Hawk and John followed her. The sky was clouding over. Nikki worried that it might storm. She checked the weather on her phone when they were at a stoplight and saw that there was a system blowing in, but no snow predicted yet. The streets were already white from yesterday's snow, and the cars left a black, wet trail behind them accented by the streetlights.

chapter nine

John pulled into the station parking lot right behind Nikki. She was a little relieved because half of her wondered if he would panic and try to flee. Once inside, Hawk and Nikki led John to the chief's office. The chief looked up from his desk.

"Hi, Chief," Hawk said. "This is John Hammer. He is Kim's boyfriend. I questioned him a bit at the apartment, but I wanted to ask him some more questions and follow up on some things he has told us. Can we use one of the rooms?"

"Yes," said the chief. "You can use the first room."

John followed Hawk down to the interrogation room. He explained the room would give them the most privacy and was equipped with a microphone for recording. Nikki realized he did not want to tell John it was an interrogation room, perhaps so he would let his guard down. Hawk told John to have a seat and asked if he wanted anything to drink.

"Yes, please. Some water?" John asked.

Nikki went down the hall to the break room and got a bottle of water. She walked back and handed it to John.

"I am going to turn you over to the chief. He will be in shortly to question you some more."

"Okay," said John, sipping on the water. He seemed a bit anxious, but Nikki was not sure if it was because he had just lost Kim and was dazed with shock, or because he knew something more about her death.

Hawk and Nikki walked out of the room and shut the door. Nikki voiced her reservations to Hawk, and he agreed with her. They went to find the chief. The chief was still in his office. Hawk went in and asked if he would continue to question John.

"Of course," said the chief, rising from his chair. "Remind me, how come we did not know about John before?"

"He had a falling out with Susan. She told Kim not to bring him to the wedding. We had not gotten to Kim's apartment yet, and no one thought to mention him to us last night," Hawk explained. He filled his father in on what John had told them about his work with addiction counseling. "I want to take a look at his office," Hawk said, and the chief agreed.

"I will go with you," Nikki insisted.

"Would you mind keeping an eye on him, maybe delay him until we get back?" Hawk asked the chief. The chief said he would sit with John and if anything else came up, he would call Hawk.

"Do you want to ride over together?" Hawk asked Nikki.

"Sure. Do you want to drive?" she asked.

"Yes, I would be happy to," he said. They got into his truck and went to John's office.

John's office was an hour away. The ride over was uneventful. The roads were slippery but not too icy. The town was lit up for Valentine's Day. Hawk and Nikki drove through the square. There were hearts on the lanterns along their main street. Hawk followed the directions to John's office. It was in a small brick building that was not well lit, a one-story office on the edge of the run-down side of town.

"Maybe he needed to have his office close to his clients," Nikki commented, voicing what they were both thinking. Hawk nodded as he parked and locked his truck. He and Nikki walked toward the building. Nikki stopped and pointed next to the front door where two men sat uneasily on a bench. They looked twitchy and angry. Nikki pegged them as drug addicts. Their clothes were filthy and they looked like they had lived a lifetime acting tough. The men looked at them sideways but scattered when Hawk moved his coat and showed them his gun.

He and Nikki walked into the building. It was hot inside, as if the winter heating was blasting. The door opened up into a small hallway. There was a worn-down upholstered bench on the side wall that Nikki would not want to sit on. There were no pictures on the wall. Across from the bench was a heavyset woman sitting at a small desk. She had a small plant that was struggling to survive in the oppressive atmosphere. The receptionist was typing on her computer and looked up when they walked in.

"May I help you? The doctor is not seeing new patients right now," she said. She was an older woman with black hair that was fading to gray at the temples. She seemed to be wearing a permanent scowl.

Nikki coughed and looked at Hawk. He put on a nice smile and leaned toward the receptionist.

"Hello, I am detective Hawk Daily, and this is my assistant Nikki Bates. We are here on behalf of the Maple Hills police department. We are conducting an investigation and we need to ask you some questions."

The receptionist asked for some identification. Hawk showed her his badge, and Nikki showed the receptionist her driver's license. The receptionist found this satisfactory and buzzed them in a door beside the desk. Hawk and Nikki stepped through and the receptionist led them to a conference room. The office hallway was narrow and crowded with dusty cardboard boxes of files, and the boxes appeared to be falling apart. The conference room had a medium-sized table and four chairs. Everyone took a chair, and Hawk started asking questions.

"So, you work for John Hammer?"

The secretary cringed. "He goes by John Jackson here," she said. She looked around as if to make sure no one had heard Hawk. They were alone in the building. *I suppose you can't be too cautious*, thought Nikki.

"Why are you asking me about him?" the receptionist asked Hawk with a strange look on her face.

"Who else would I be asking you about?"

"Usually if police come in here, they are trying to get information on one of our clients. Our clients are not rich people with Beverly Hills addictions, Detective. Our clients are on a first-name basis with the police – and not in a good way. The cops show up about once a week asking if one of our clients has missed any mandated counseling sessions. I have never had anyone in here ask about John," she insisted.

"How long has John been in this office?" Hawk asked.

"Dr. Jackson has been renting this office for six years."

"And remind us about the services he provides?"

"He is a rehabilitation psychologist. He helps people who are addicted to various drugs. Sometimes they are court-appointed clients and some just walk in off the streets. John talks to them and counsels them on more productive ways to handle their addictions. He is not a psychiatrist. He does not dispense any medication, just counseling," the receptionist said. "Is Dr. Jackson in some kind of trouble?" Despite the fact that she knew his real name, and knew that they knew, the receptionist insisted on using his alibi. *She is trained well,* thought Nikki.

"Why would you ask that?" Hawk asked.

"Because you are here asking questions about him," the receptionist responded abruptly.

"No, he is not in any trouble; we are just following up on some things he told us. Do you know if John is seeing anyone romantically?"

"I have no idea," she replied. "He keeps his business and personal lives separate."

"So, you were not aware that his girlfriend died?" Nikki asked.

The receptionist inhaled quickly. "No. I did not even know he was seeing anyone. Bless him, poor John. Dr. Jackson always insisted we keep our personal lives private, well away from the clients during business hours. He never told me anything about a girlfriend. He would come into work, take a break for lunch, and then finish the day. He never went anywhere. He brought his food from home. He was in the building from 8-5 every single work day."

"Would you mind if we took a look in John's office?"

"Well, do not mess anything up," the receptionist replied. "There are some sensitive files in there. I do not want you to look through the files as we have to follow confidentiality laws for his patients."

"Okay," said Hawk. "We will stay out of the files for now."

The receptionist showed them to John's office. It was small. Inside were a desk and two chairs, one in front of the desk and one behind it. There was a computer on the desk and a filing cabinet along the wall. Hawk thanked the receptionist, and she went back to her desk. Nikki looked around. The walls were bare. There were no pictures or degrees hanging anywhere. The walls were industrial wood paneling. They had been painted a dark, depressing brown. The floor was worn, speckled linoleum tile, the kind you might see in a school cafeteria. Or a prison, she shuddered. She imagined sitting here all day and shivered.

Nikki looked at the desk. All of the paperwork listed Dr. John Jackson. There was no mention of John Hammer anywhere. If she did not know about the alias, she would have thought she was in the wrong office. Nikki turned on the computer, but she was locked out. She did not want to mess with trying to break the password at the moment. Meanwhile, Hawk was looking in a filing cabinet. There were files in alphabetical order, but nothing useful. Nikki sat in the desk chair and looked over the desk. There were more files, paper pads, and a marble paperweight. She looked through the stack of files quickly but did not see anything of note.

"Have you found anything?" Hawk asked.

"No. There is nothing here," Nikki said, frustrated. Perhaps he really was exactly what he seemed – a good boyfriend who just happened to have a strange job. She put her purse on the desk and got out her phone. Frustrated that they had made the long drive for nothing, she figured she better text Seth to see how things were coming at the store. The phone slipped out of her hand and fell under the desk.

Nikki sighed, pushed back the chair, and leaned down to get it. She maneuvered under the desk and got her phone. She looked up to make sure she did not bump her head on the drawer on the way out. Suddenly she stopped. "Hawk, come see this."

He got down on his hands and knees and looked where Nikki was pointing. On the bottom of the desk drawer was another hidden drawer with a small lock. From the top, it could not be seen. Nikki moved out from under the desk to let Hawk get a better look with his flashlight. Hawk tried to open it, but it would not budge. He looked at Nikki. Nikki smiled and looked in her purse. She pulled out a small box and handed it to Hawk.

"This might help," she suggested.

Hawk took the box and opened it. There were lock-picking tools inside – after all of her casual sleuthing, she had finally invested in a set. Hawk grinned. He put the tools in the lock and jimmied it open and pulled out the contents. He laid them on the top of the desk. There was a passport and a couple of pictures.

"What are these doing here?" Nikki wondered.

The pictures were of John, but he was not with Kim. He was with another woman. They seemed to be happy. They were both smiling and holding hands. There was a desert in the background of one picture and a forest in the background of another. Nikki picked up the passport. It was unexpired. It had John's real name and a photo of him staring into the camera with his recognizable blond hair. As she thumbed through it, she noticed stamps from Mexico and Brazil. She looked at Hawk, and they gathered this evidence into a pile. Hawk called the chief.

"Is John still there?" he asked.

"Yes, but he asked if he could leave soon."

"Try to get him to stay; we need to ask him some more questions. New evidence has come to light, and we are not sure how it ties into the case. We'll show you when we get back. Delay him any way you can."

The chief agreed to delay John. Hawk put the pictures and passport into an evidence bag and put the bag in Nikki's purse while she packed up her lock-picking tools. They put the chair back under the desk and walked out into the reception area. Hawk thanked the receptionist on their way out. She barely looked up as they passed her desk. Once they were out of the office area proper, Nikki glanced back and saw her get up to check the office. *She probably thinks we snooped in the patient files.*

Nikki and Hawk walked back to the truck. Nikki looked

around but did not see the two men from before. She breathed easier and got into Hawk's truck.

"We have to get back there before John tries to leave," Nikki said.

"Yes." Hawk said grimly. "He's going to get suspicious soon." He started the truck and turned on his blue and white lights. They raced down the road back to Maple Hills.

chapter ten

When Nikki and Hawk were close to the station, Nikki's phone rang. It was Seth.

"I heard from my friend. He said that yes, John and Kim have been seeing each other for a while," Seth said.

"Thank you. We are just getting to the station. Can I call you back later?" Nikki asked.

"Yes. Take care, Mom."

"I will, you too," she answered. Nikki told Hawk what Seth had told her. Hawk agreed that it was good to have some corroboration to John's story. That still did not explain the pictures and passport. Hawk pulled into a parking space near the station. He got out and opened Nikki's door. He held her hand so she would not slip on the icy sidewalk.

They went into the station and the officer at the desk told them the chief was still in with John. Nikki breathed a sigh of relief. *He is still here.* She and Hawk walked quickly down the hallway. They got to the interrogation room and opened the door. The chief was sitting across from John, and he stood up when the door opened. The remains of two donuts were scattered across two napkins.

"I told him you had some more questions. He agreed to

wait for you because I told him we still had at least one chocolate glazed left in the breakroom," the chief told Hawk with a wink.

"Thank you, Chief."

"I have some work to do in my office. He is all yours," replied the chief. He walked out and shut the door. Hawk walked over to the table.

"Nikki, would you please give me what we found in John's office?" Hawk asked Nikki.

"With pleasure," she said and pulled the evidence bag out of her purse.

"What is that?" John asked.

"That's what we were going to ask you," replied Hawk. He opened the bag and laid the pictures and passport on the table in front of John.

John looked closer and turned pale. "Where did you find those?" John demanded in a soft tone.

"In the underside of your desk drawer," Hawk replied. "Who is that in the pictures and where were they taken? Why were you hiding them?"

John's shoulders slumped down. He put his head in his hand, and Nikki could tell he was crying. She walked over and sat down across the table from him. Hawk stood behind her, and they waited for John to regain his composure. John picked up his head.

"That is my former wife," he explained to Hawk and Nikki. "Those pictures were taken in Mexico and Brazil on our honeymoon. We stayed in Brazil for a week and then returned to Mexico."

"That is your former wife?" Nikki prodded.

"Yes. I was married to Alexa, the woman in the photos. We were happily married and then she died. I did not realize she was an addict when we got married. By the time I realized it, she was evidently too far gone. She died of an overdose."

Nikki looked at Hawk and raised her eyebrow.

"Go on," encouraged Hawk to John.

"I had traveled to Mexico to help addicts. I wanted to set up a clinic there. I met Alexa while I was looking for a building to rent. She was a realtor, and she found an office I could use. I set up my clinic and helped many patients there. Alexa and I grew close. She would volunteer at the clinic, and I got to know her. I proposed to her, and we got married. We were happy and in love. She was smart, sexy, and talkative. We complemented each other. I never knew she had a dark secret she was hiding from me. I have helped many addicts. I never knew I was married to one. She kept that secret hidden well. The day before she died, I found her stash. I gave her an ultimatum: get help or get out. She denied using, but I told her the evidence was right in front of me. I wanted to help her desperately, but unless she consented to my help there was nothing I could do. I stayed at a friend's house that night. The next day she was dead. She overdosed during the night." He closed his eyes for a moment in pain. After a moment, he continued. "I went into a tailspin and left Mexico. I am originally from Maple Hills, so I decided to come back to the states and start a practice here. I found the building you were clearly just in. It was close to where a lot of addicts squat in abandoned houses. I wanted them to be able to walk to the clinic if they had to. I met Kim five years ago. She was a wonderful woman who loved me for who I was. She knew about my former wife and my time in Mexico. Despite my mistakes, she loved me anyway. I kept the pictures in my desk because I did not want Kim to run across them in the apartment. I left my passport there because I thought it would be safe. I did not think anyone would find it."

Hawk thanked him for explaining. He asked John to stay a little longer. John agreed, slumping again as if the story had taken all his energy.

Hawk and Nikki left the room and went to talk to the

chief. They found him in his office looking at something on his computer.

"Well, what did he have to say?" asked the chief when they walked in.

"He said the pictures were of him and his former wife," said Hawk. "He said that Kim knew about her, but we cannot confirm that. He also said his former wife died of a drug overdose."

The chief looked up, startled. "Another woman this man was with died from an overdose? I would like to keep him here for a while. I do not trust him. I need to verify some things, and I will continue to question him."

"I agree," said Hawk and he looked over at Nikki.

"He lied to his patients about who he really is. Even if he was doing it to keep himself separated from them, it is still a lie. His wife died of an overdose, and now Kim is dead from an overdose. I think you have enough evidence to justify holding him until we can figure things out," Nikki said.

"Well, at least now I can call the mayor and tell him we have a suspect in custody. He will be happy to hear that," said the chief.

"Susan and Tim deserve to know, too," suggested Nikki. "I guess Susan won't be happy to know she was right about Kim's boyfriend, though."

"Well, I would like to be sure he is the one who did it," said Hawk. "Until then, we are not certain what exactly is going on. If he did not do it, are Susan and Tim safe?" he asked.

"That is a good point. Why don't you and Nikki attend the wedding and mingle with the guests. You can keep an eye on Susan, Tim, and the bridal party."

"That is a good idea," said Nikki.

"I agree," said Hawk.

"Okay. Let me call the mayor, and I will make arrangements for you to attend."

"Actually, Susan invited all of us the other day. She was so grateful that I could deliver chocolates for the wedding and reception on such short notice that she told me to bring Hawk and the whole crew."

"That is perfect," said the chief. "I will fill the mayor in on what is happening. At least he will stop breathing down my neck. I just hope he is too busy to hold a press conference."

"I'm going to go and check out the shop," said Nikki.

"I will do a bit of research and then pick you up for the wedding," said Hawk to Nikki.

"Okay. I will be at my house soon," she replied.

Nikki walked out of the precinct and down the street towards her shop. She thought about what John had told them. Things did not look good for John.

She rounded the corner and her heart lifted to see her shop waiting for her. She went in the front door. Seth and Tori were there, along with Lidia. There was about an hour until closing time. Nikki walked in and said hello. There was one customer left, and Tori was just giving him his change. He thanked Tori and smiled at Nikki when he left. Nikki sat down at a table, and Seth joined her.

"The day was a success," exclaimed Seth. "We set up the chocolates and the fountain at the venue. Madeline was thrilled with the display, though she did ask if you were planning to check in with her. And we had a record number of customers at the shop today. We have almost sold out of the chocolate-covered strawberries."

"That is fantastic," Nikki replied.

"How is the case coming?" asked Lidia.

"We have a suspect in custody," said Nikki. Everyone looked at her.

"Who is it?" asked Seth and Tori at the same time.

"It is John, Kim's boyfriend."

"That is awful," said Tori.

"Yes, it is," replied Nikki. "Please do not tell anyone.

Hawk wants this to stay under wraps until the investigation is over. John is still just a suspect. We still have a lot of work to do on the case."

"Absolutely, I would hate for the case to go wrong just because one of us said the wrong thing to someone," agreed Lidia. Seth and Tori agreed not to tell anyone.

"Well, I am going to run by the venue and check out the table. The last thing I need is Madeline getting frustrated with me. Then I plan to go home and get ready for the wedding. You can close the shop a bit early, that way you can get ready too," she told Lidia. Lidia agreed, and Nikki said she would see everyone at the wedding.

In her car, Nikki navigated the roads that were slippery from the previous day's snow. She reflected that this had been one of the longest days of her life, but luckily, they had turned up a likely suspect in time to please the mayor and save Chief Daily's job. At the venue, she hurried toward the back door, anxious to finish this last detail so she could finally go home and get ready for the big event.

chapter eleven

I f the reception hall had been bustling the evening of the rehearsal dinner, tonight there were even more people, all hurrying around but nimbly avoiding each other. Nikki passed through the kitchens and went into the front of the hall. All of the decorations from the rehearsal dinner had been taken down and replaced with swaths of creamy white satin. The wedding planner had turned the hall into a shimmery white fantasy, like a winter palace. There were small mirror balls hanging and reflecting light around the room. White roses lined the wall, and the bride's table was white and pink. There were snowy white cloths on the tables and silver settings, with tasteful, pale pink chargers under each place setting. Nikki's chocolate table was in the corner. The chocolate fountain stood out against all the whiteness, and her fruits looked even more like jewels in the glittery spectacle of the decorative motif. She adjusted a few trays to better catch the light, but otherwise the table looked perfect. Nikki saw Madeline and walked over to her.

"Everything looks beautiful," Nikki exclaimed.

"Thank you. I hope Susan and her family feel the same way."

"I am sure they will be as impressed as I am," Nikki reassured her.

"Well, if I can pull this off, I hope to be able to expand my client base. All the who's-who of Maple Hills will be here."

"That's what the mayor told me," said Nikki.

"Your chocolates look incredible," said Madeline.

"Thank you."

"Oh here, let me give you this," Madeline handed Nikki one of her cards. Nikki looked at her questioningly.

"Why are you handing me this?"

"I saw who you walked in with last night and how he looked at you. Trust me, you will be needing my services soon."

Nikki blushed and laughed. She thanked Madeline and put the card in her wallet. *Not that I will be needing this anytime soon, but it is polite to take something that is offered to you,* she thought.

"Well, it is time for me to go home and get changed," Nikki said, trying to think of a way to politely escape.

"Yes, I think your table has been given the final approval. I will see you later," Madeline said, giving her a quick wave. Nikki walked outside to her car, relieved. She sat down and started the car. She realized she had not picked out her dress the night before. With the adrenaline of the investigation, it had been the last thing on her mind.

She rushed home and looked through her closet. Seth had already left to pick up Tori, so she had to trust her instincts on this outfit. Nikki found the dress she was looking for. It was a long, formal, asymmetrical dress with one flowing sleeve and the other side cut away to expose her shoulder. The dress was emerald green, and she had matching heels with a rhinestone-and-pearl accent at the toes. Nikki showered and styled her hair carefully in an elegant but loose bun, then slid into the silky dress and stepped into her heels. She didn't often get to dress up this fancy, and it was fun. She was just finishing her makeup when she heard the front door open.

"I am up here. I will be down in a minute," she called.

"Okay, I will wait in the kitchen," Hawk replied. "Do you have any coffee?"

"Yes, I put a pot on when I got home. There should be some left." Nikki finished her makeup and put on her earrings, a pair that draped in graceful loops of diamond against her neck. Nikki walked down the stairs, and Hawk whistled.

Hawk walked towards her and put his arms around Nikki. He gave her a kiss.

"You look spectacular," he said. "Susan will be angry with you."

"Why?" asked Nikki, smiling.

"Everyone will be looking at you and not her."

Nikki laughed and gently punched his arm. "You look handsome, yourself," she told Hawk. His formal suit made him look handsome as ever and showed off his strong arms. He thanked her with a grin and asked if she was ready to go.

"Yes, just let me get my wrap." Nikki had splurged and bought a matching faux fur wrap for her dress.

"Are you sure you will be warm in that?" asked Hawk.

Nikki laughed. "Yes, it is heavy. Also, the tent will be heated."

"That's right," said Hawk. He took her arm and led her to his truck. He helped her get in and closed the door.

They drove into town and parked by the center of town. Hawk took Nikki's arm and escorted her to the wedding tent. There were special portable heaters disguised as old-fashioned lampposts stationed all around the tents to keep the guests warm. White and red hearts hung all around. There were white glittery snowflakes on the trees and fairy lights shone all around. Nikki looked around and spotted

Seth and Tori. They were with Lidia and her husband. Seth saw her and waved.

"It looks like the crew saved us some seats," Nikki told Hawk. They walked over and sat down.

"You look beautiful," Tori gushed to Nikki.

"You look pretty, too," Nikki said. Tori had on a short flowered dress that clung to her figure in a flattering way. It had gathered sleeves down to the elbow and a sweetheart neckline. Seth was handsome next to her in his tuxedo.

Lidia had on a formal but more practical flowered chiffon skirt and a pink blouse. She wore gloves and looked sharp. Her husband was in a tuxedo, also. Nikki looked around and admired how pretty everything looked.

"Did you get a chance to stop by the venue?" Seth asked.

"Yes. The table was set up perfectly," Nikki replied.

"Good. I think Tori and I will leave as soon as the wedding is done so we can get the fountain started and pull the plastic wrap off the candies."

"Thank you. I really appreciate your help," said Nikki. Just then, the music started. A little girl walked down the aisle in a cute pink dress. She was throwing flower petals in front of her and the crowd cooed to see how adorable she was. The bridesmaids followed in light pink A-line dresses and stood at the altar next to the handsomely attired groomsmen.

Becky, Susan's maid of honor, walked down the aisle after the bridesmaids in a hot pink A-line dress. The color complemented her. Once Becky was stationed next to the best man at the front of the tent, the music changed, and everyone stood up in anticipation.

Nikki and Hawk used this opportunity to scan the crowd more thoroughly, but no one stood out or looked unusual. The mayor and Susan appeared. He was proudly beaming, and she was glowing in her wedding dress, which had a lace bodice and flowed down with a cascade of fluttering tiers to a small train. The neckline left her shoulders bare and a beautiful veil covered her hair. They walked down the aisle together and up to the front of the tent.

The minister was waiting there, and as the music stopped, everyone sat down. Nikki and Hawk continued to scan the crowd throughout the ceremony, but things went smoothly. *I wonder if we do have the right suspect*, Nikki thought. Hawk nudged her and pointed out Chief Daily and a few plainclothes policemen in the crowd. Nikki was glad for their presence. Everyone seemed happy, but there was a bit of an edge to the ceremony, after the events of last night. The couple said their "I do's" and kissed. Everyone in the audience clapped and cheered.

To more cheers and the flashes of many cameras, the happy couple went back down the aisle to a waiting limo that would take them to the reception, and the guests began to exit to their cars. Seth and Tori left to prepare the chocolate table. Nikki and Hawk stayed behind and made sure nothing happened to the wedding party or any of the guests. When the last guest had left, Hawk led Nikki to his truck. He helped her in and they went to the reception. The lot was full by then, so Hawk dropped Nikki in front of the building and parked the truck. Nikki waited for him and they went in together.

The hall was buzzing with conversation. The wedding party was seated at their table and the reception was in full swing. Nikki and Hawk found their table. Her crew was already there, as was the chief. Appetizers were being served. Nikki looked at Susan. She was glowing. She actually seemed a bit more relaxed. Nikki was happy for her.

As Nikki and Hawk nibbled on their appetizers, Hawk filled his father in on the uneventful exit of all the guests from the tent.

"Do you have people here?" Hawk asked the chief.

"Yes, most of the precinct is here, as a matter of fact. See that waitress?"

Nikki looked where the chief was pointing. She saw a blonde waitress and smiled. Nikki recognized Judy from the precinct. She noticed a few others, but they blended in well.

"Where is John?" Hawk asked the chief.

"I decided to keep him overnight. Because his first wife died of an overdose, I could not let him go. If he is our killer, I did not want him anywhere near this wedding."

Hawk nodded in agreement. Nikki relaxed a bit, knowing that John was being held. After the appetizers, the main course appeared. It was surf and turf. Everyone had filet and lobster tail. The chief leaned over to Nikki.

"The mayor said he had these flown in yesterday, fresh from the ocean." Nikki smiled. *Of course he did*, she thought.

"It looks wonderful," she said. It tasted wonderful, too. After dinner, the wedding party roamed around the room thanking their guests. Everyone was invited to have some chocolate and a line formed at Nikki's chocolate table. Nikki heard some ooh's and ahh's. She smiled, happy that everyone seemed to like the dessert. Hawk squeezed her hand.

"Another success from Nikki's chocolate factory," he teased.

"I think everyone likes it," Tori said, looking at the long line that had formed.

"Look how much the mayor took," said Lidia, laughing at the piled-high plate. Nikki and Hawk laughed, too. Not long after that, the band started playing, and the groom took his wife out for the first dance, and then the mayor came out for a dance with his daughter, too. The wedding party joined in. The next song had even more people on the dance floor. Hawk and Nikki danced together, and Nikki relaxed in his arms. They danced awhile, forgetting their cares and even forgetting their lack of sleep in the last couple days.

When it was time to cut the cake, everyone crowded

around the cake table. The cake was four layers high, decorated in white and pink rose petals, and had white chocolate chips inside. There were champagne toasts after everyone had a piece, and then it was finally nearing the end of the night – Susan and Tim announced they were leaving. The guests piled outside to wave goodbye on the front steps. The best man drove Tim's car around to the front. There were tin cans tied to the back and "The Happy Couple" was written on the rear window. Tim and Susan laughed. The guests threw birdseed at them as they dashed toward the car. They sped off into the frosty night, and then the guests started to disperse.

Nikki started to feel tired, finally. But she knew they still had more to go over. Seth offered to drop off Tori and drive Nikki home. She agreed. She gave Hawk a kiss and told him to meet them after he got changed. Hawk agreed and walked to his truck.

Later at the house, Nikki and Seth changed out of their party clothes in favor of warm sweatpants and sweaters. Nikki made hot chocolate and on the way home, they had picked up the last of the chocolate-covered strawberries from the chocolate shop. She and Seth were sitting in the den by the fire when the front door opened and Hawk walked in.

"Look who I found outside," he said. Tori walked in with him. Seth got up and kissed her hello. Nikki told Hawk to get some hot chocolate and join them in the den. Hawk got a mug for Tori and himself and brought them into the den. He handed Tori her mug and sat down by Nikki. They talked about the wedding, and Nikki relaxed into Hawk's shoulder. She was getting drifty when Hawk's phone rang. He looked at it and told Nikki it was the chief.

"Hello," he said. "What is happening? Okay, we will be right there."

Hawk jumped up to grab his coat. Nikki asked what was happening.

"I'm not sure. Something's going on at the precinct and dad says he needs us there right away."

"Okay," said Nikki. "Seth, you and Tori stay here. I will let you know what is going on as soon as possible." Seth meanwhile had leaped up, too.

"I'm coming with you," he declared.

"No," said Nikki. "Stay here with Tori."

"I know you are worried, Mom, but I can handle myself under pressure. I don't want to get stranded out here, wondering if you're okay, if you forget to pick up your phone again."

Nikki knew he was right. She looked at Hawk.

"Okay, but stay close," Hawk warned. "I do not want you to get hurt."

Seth promised to stay close, and Tori said she would stay at the house in case Lidia called or came over. Nikki, Hawk, and Seth piled in Hawk's truck. Hawk drove quickly to the station, barreling down through the twisty, hilly roads as fast as he dared.

In town, Hawk headed for the station, and from the flashing police lights reflecting off the nearby buildings, they knew something was up before they even rounded the corner. As they parked, they saw that the station was surrounded by police, and there were spotlights trained on the front entrance. A man was talking on a megaphone. They quickly found the chief and asked what was going on.

"A man walked in with a gun and demanded to see John," the chief said. "The deputy at the front desk was unarmed when he came in, though at least he was able to sound the alarm. Most of us were able to get out, but John is still inside. There are only two deputies in there with him, he's been threatening Deputy Smith at the front desk for the past ten minutes."

Nikki looked in the front window. She saw a man holding a gun. He was pointing it at one of the deputies. Evidently the discussion had gone from bad to worse, because then they could hear him yelling at the man, demanding to see John. The deputy said he could not take the gunman into the back of the precinct building. The gunman shot the wall behind the deputy, and there was an angry, tense murmur from the crowd of officers watching from the parking lot. The gunman demanded the deputy give him his gun. The deputy complied. The gunman then put his gun to Deputy Smith's head, pulled him out of the seat, and demanded the deputy take him to see John. The gunman and deputy disappeared from view.

"We have to go after him," Hawk said. "We need to breach the building."

"No," said the chief. He didn't say it out loud, but he was reluctant to risk his son in a dangerous situation. "Let me send a couple of deputies."

"I am better trained in SWAT tactics than your deputies, and Nikki and I know each other well," Hawk countered. The chief resisted again but finally agreed to Hawk's plan. Nikki told Seth to stay with the chief, and then she and Hawk started running in a crouch to the side of the building.

chapter twelve

Hawk and Nikki ducked and ran across the snow-covered lawn to the side of the building. They both reached the wall and slid closer to the nearest door. Hawk reviewed a few standard law enforcement SWAT hand signals with Nikki so there would be no confusion inside. She listened and memorized them, though she was already familiar with most of them. They were ready to go.

Hawk and Nikki entered the building by the side door. Hawk went first and cleared the corridor, and Nikki covered him. They moved quickly and methodically, checking the back hallways and offices. The building was quiet. In one room, a woman was sitting in a corner behind a desk. Hawk told her she could go out the back door. She thanked him and ran out quietly. Hawk and Nikki moved through the next few rooms, clearing the rooms and their lines of sight as they went.

Hawk rounded the corner and ducked behind a desk. They were next to the interview room where John had been held and could hear voices from inside. The desk was across from the door to the interview room and its bulk provided good cover. Hawk held up his hand and motioned Nikki to follow him. Nikki moved quickly and quietly beside him and crouched behind the desk. Hawk looked over the desk carefully and scanned the interview room. He ducked back down behind the desk. He told Nikki that the deputies who had been guarding John were tied up in a corner. John was seated in a chair. The gunman had the deputies' weapons beside him on the ground. The gunman could not see Hawk and Nikki, but they could hear what he was saying to John.

"I finally have you," he said, pacing in front of John.

"Who are you?" John asked.

"You know who I am. I am the one who scared off the villagers around your little clinic in Mexico. Those people were moving my drugs. You were in my way. You tried to get rid of me, but you failed. I lived in the village for years before you came along. Don't you understand how the world works? The villagers all knew who I was – they all worked for me, and in return, I did not kill them. I used them as mules to get my drugs across the border. Some of them made it, and some did not. Those who made it back received a bonus. They were my favorites. They could slip past the border patrols and the customs inspectors and deliver the goods to California. Your former wife, Alexa, was one of my best mules."

John tried to get up, but the gunman pressed his weapon into John's head at the temple, forcing him back down into his chair.

"What are you talking about?" John asked him angrily. "My wife was not a drug mule."

The gunman laughed. "Oh, yes she was. Because no one suspected her, she got away with it. She fit in with the crowd of tourists and vacationers. She seemed so sweet and innocent, yes?" he leered. "She was anything but."

John tried to move again. The gunman warned him with another cruel gesture to stay still.

"How could you know my wife? She never mentioned you. She would have told me if she had been running drugs. I found drugs in our house...but it was a single dose. If she was running them, there would have been more. My wife died of an accidental drug overdose," said John, his voice half desperate and half angry.

"Really? Is that what the medical examiner told you?" sneered the gunman.

"Yes. I found her stash the night before she died. When I got home the next day, she was dead."

"She did not die accidentally. Believe me, it was no accident when I injected that heroin into her neck. She struggled, but like all good junkies, she enjoyed it before she passed out and died."

"What are you talking about?" John yelled. "Why would you do that?"

"I did it because I found out you were working undercover for the cops. I told Alexa, but she refused to believe me. After Alexa met you, she refused to run any more drugs. Even when I told her you were working with the police, she refused to listen. *I* planted those drugs for you to find. I thought you would kick her out and finally knock some sense into her. If you had, she would still be alive. She would have come running back to me. But no, she insisted she was in love. I could not have my best mule living with an undercover cop."

"I don't know what you're talking about. I'm a psychologist! I ran a clinic in Mexico. I am not a cop. Alexa and I were happy together. We just wanted to be married and live in peace," John insisted, pleading again.

"What? You don't think I have proof? You think I would kill Alexa on a suspicion? When I suspected something was not right, I had my men follow you. They took pictures of you meeting with the American DEA and the task force from the Mexican government. Here, I'll show them to you." The gunman pulled out a stack of pictures from his front jacket pocket, never taking his gun off of John. He threw the pictures in John's lap. "Pick them up and look at them. Tell me I am wrong."

John looked down at the pictures and turned pale. He did not pick them up.

"But Alexa's death wasn't enough of a warning for you, was it? After you left Mexico, they raided my warehouses. They took everything from me. I evaded capture and ran from the police. You thought you'd escaped scot-free and left me to hang for my crimes, but I swore I would track you down and have my revenge. I found you and took the life of your new woman. She was pretty when I found her, all dolled up for the wedding. That pink dress. Her pretty hair. What a shame."

"You killed Kim?" John yelled. "I will kill you," he threatened the gunman.

"No. You won't kill me. You will die here tonight, I promise. Then you can be with both the women you loved," the gunman threatened.

"How did you kill Kim?" John asked.

"I have been watching you both for a couple of weeks. I heard about her friend's wedding, and I decided that I would take advantage of the festivities. When I heard there was a rehearsal dinner, I found a waiter's uniform. I slipped into the back of the venue when everyone was dancing. I told her there was a phone call for her. Silly, naïve girl. She believed me. She followed me down the hall. I pulled her aside and took her out to my van. She put up a bit of a struggle, but I got the injection in her right away. A massive dose. I waited until the heroin had kicked in enough to make her seem drunk, and I led her back to the party. I let the drugs do their work. No one saw me. Everyone was too busy working or having fun. Her friends thought she had been drinking and was rambling nonsense, and they stuck her at a table. I knew better. It was not long after that when she passed out. I knew she would be dead within minutes, so I left. It was easy."

John tried to get up again, but the gunman held him down with an arm across his chest. The gunman put his gun to John's head and cocked the trigger. Nikki looked at Hawk. She whispered, "We have to do something." Hawk nodded. Nikki felt along the edge of the desk and brought her hand back down. She was holding a pen. She motioned throwing it, and Hawk smiled and nodded.

Nikki tossed the pen behind the gunman. He turned to look where the noise was coming from. Before he could turn back, John jumped out of the chair and tackled him. Nikki and Hawk jumped up and Hawk leaped over the desk to help take down the gunman. John hit the gunman in the face and slammed the gunman's hand on the tile floor. The man dropped the gun, and Nikki kicked it away. Hawk had the man on his stomach, his hands wrenched behind his back, in mere seconds. He cuffed the gunman and hauled him to his feet. With one respectful nod at John, Hawk took the gunman down to a jailcell before letting the chief and the others know everything was clear.

Nikki freed the deputies and turned to John. "Was all that true?" she asked in disbelief.

"Yes. I worked for the DEA in Mexico. We tried to take down his operation, he was part of a big cartel that controlled the whole coastline. I was so distraught over Alexa I had to leave before the takedown was even finished. The DEA asked me to set up a clinic here to try and make progress tracking the cartel's distributions in the states. I agreed and was making some progress right before Kim died. I think I have enough on him to put him away for good now. The DEA will come and get him soon, I suppose."

The chief had come inside.

"Good work, Nikki," he said. "Hawk told me what the gunman said, John. Is there a number I can call to verify that you worked with the DEA?"

John gave the chief his contact name and number. The

chief called the number and verified the information. When the chief got off the phone, he shook hands with John and apologized for ever doubting him.

"The DEA said they would send someone over to pick up the gunman. They should be here in about half an hour," he informed John.

"Thank you. I understand why you took me in. If I was in your shoes, I would have doubted me, too. I never wanted anyone to get hurt. I opened the clinic here to work with the local addicts and dealers. We were trying to bring down the cartel once and for all. I couldn't compromise my identity."

"Was Kim aware of what you were really doing?"

"Yes, and she supported me. She knew the risks, but she wanted to be with me anyway. She was a very strong woman." John sat down. He looked exhausted and wiped out. The chief handed him some coffee. Hawk returned from locking up the gunman, and Nikki filled him in. Hawk apologized to John and shook his hand.

Nikki and Hawk were both astounded by the evening's events. Seth joined them in Hawk's office and told them he was psyched to see justice in action. Law enforcement was one of his career interests. Nikki hugged him and was glad he had gotten the rare chance to see another branch of law enforcement doing their job, and during a hostage situation no less. She felt badly for John, though. *No one should lose the one they love like that,* she thought.

"So, would you like to stay at my place?" Nikki asked Hawk. "You're my ride home, but you're welcome to stay. It's so late now. You are welcome to come along, too. We have a guest bed," she offered to John. John thanked her but said he just wanted to go home and get some rest. He said he would wait for the other agents to pick up the gunman. The chief said he would see that John got back home safely. Nikki nodded in understanding.

Hawk agreed to stay over, and he drove Nikki and Seth

back home. Tori was waiting for them with some light snacks she had whipped up while they were gone. There were plates with sandwiches on them and some macaroni and cheese. It was very late and a chilly wind was blowing in the dark night as they hurried into the warm house. Nikki was glad to come home to some homemade food and a warm fire. "Tori, you're a lifesaver," Nikki said as she sat down in the den.

"I hear you saved some lives tonight too, Nikki," Tori commented, her eyes wide as Seth had shared the details as soon as they had returned.

Hawk grinned and went into the kitchen to make a plate to share with Nikki. He carried it into the den with two forks and handed one to Nikki. Nikki thanked him and snuggled up with him on the sofa. Seth and Tori sat on the love seat, and they all watched the fire and enjoyed their meal. Nikki told Hawk he could sleep on the sofa, and Seth offered Tori his room. He said he would sleep in the den, since there was an extra air mattress in the closet.

"It's a sleepover party," Nikki laughed. Everyone laughed with her. But her laughter turned quickly into a massive yawn, and Nikki stretched and announced she was going to bed. She helped Hawk make up the sofa while Seth changed his sheets for Tori. Seth brought down a blanket and sheets and set the air mattress up by the dwindling fire. Hawk took Nikki aside and hugged her.

"Happy Valentine's Day," he said.

Nikki smiled. "Happy Valentine's Day to you, too."

chapter thirteen

Nikki woke up early the next morning. She had intended to be the first one up so she could make breakfast for everyone. When she got up out of bed, though, she smelled coffee and bacon already wafting up the stairs. She smiled. Instead of jumping out of bed, she decided to relax in the shower and then go downstairs. After she was dressed, she went down to the kitchen. Hawk was standing at the stove making eggs, bacon, and grits. The freshly-brewed coffee was sitting on the table in a carafe. Seth and Tori were in their pajamas, sitting at the kitchen table. Nikki looked out the window. It had stopped snowing, but the sun shone brightly on the sparkling white landscape. A cardinal flew by, and a squirrel hopped across the lawn. It was a peaceful morning. Nikki walked over to Hawk and gave him a hug and kiss.

"Good morning," she said.

"Good morning to you," Hawk replied. "Do you want something for breakfast? Or everything?"

"Load up a plate," she said. Hawk smiled and dished out the food. Nikki took the plate to the table and joined Seth and Tori. Hawk made himself a plate, and they sat down together.

"I think I might open the shop a bit late today," Nikki

mused. Hawk's jaw dropped. Nikki always had the store open first thing in the morning. It had been a truly unusual Valentine's Day. Just then, there was a knock on the door.

"I'll get it," said Seth. He hopped up and went to the door. Nikki heard him say hello, and she turned around to see Lidia walking in.

"Good morning. I wanted you to know that I have made an official decision."

"What is it?" asked Nikki.

"I have closed the shop for the day."

"What? Why?" asked Nikki.

"Because, Nikki, you have done enough for this town this past week. You have worked non-stop, and you need a break. I have already put a sign on the door. Everyone who stopped by agreed with me, including the mayor."

"Well, if the mayor said to take a day off, who am I to argue?" Nikki asked. Everyone laughed.

"Have some coffee and breakfast, Lidia," Hawk offered.

"Thank you, I will," she replied, taking a seat at the table. Nikki smiled. She did deserve a break. The chocolates could keep for another day.

Everyone relaxed and enjoyed Hawk's delicious cooking. After breakfast, Nikki ordered Hawk to relax for a change. Tori and Seth cleaned up the dishes, and Nikki put them away. Lidia said she had to get back home. Her husband would be delighted to have her home for the day.

"That or he will dread the honey-do list I come up with for him." Nikki and Hawk laughed. Lidia said goodbye. Tori and Seth said they were finally going to go to that long-postponed movie. They asked if Nikki and Hawk wanted to join them. Nikki looked at Hawk.

"I thought we could take a hike," Hawk suggested.

"Yeah, I think we will do that instead. Thank you for the offer, though," Nikki said to Seth. Seth said he understood.

"We're having lunch in town after the movie, so don't wait up for us, Mom." Seth and Tori put on their coats and left.

It was quiet in the house. The beautiful outdoors was calling. Nikki went up to her room and put on her hiking boots. She grabbed her parka and went downstairs. She put on her coat and hat, and Hawk wound her scarf around her neck, carefully tucking it in so she would be warm in the chilly February winds. He took her hand and they went outside. Snow started falling, but it was light and airy. It blew around the trail in front of Nikki and Hawk. Nikki loved this kind of snow. She stuck out her tongue and caught some snowflakes. Their coldness nipped at her tongue. Hawk laughed. They walked in the woods around Nikki's house. There were worn trails from previous hikes that even the snow could not hide.

The snow was lighter in the woods, sheltered by the branches of the trees. Nikki occasionally heard a snap and a large pile of snow would come down from the trees above. The wind picked up, and the snow whirled out of the trees and started to get behind Nikki's scarf and freeze her neck. She felt the melting snow run down her back. After the third time this happened, Nikki looked at Hawk.

"I think it is time to head back to the house," she said. Her head felt clearer and lighter. She enjoyed being out in nature, and was glad Hawk was there to enjoy it with her.

"Okay. Have you gotten enough snow for the day?"

Nikki laughed. "Yes. My neck is starting to freeze." Hawk laughed. He took Nikki's hand. As they were walking back, he stopped her. He froze. Nikki looked at him and he put his finger to his lips. He pointed past one of the trees. Nikki looked and gasped. There was a deer about ten feet away. It was a buck, and he was majestic. He had been eating, but he stopped and looked at them, his antlers magnificent against the stark winter landscape. They held still. He started to pick his way slowly through the snow away from them. Nikki and

Hawk watched him go. Nikki realized she had been holding her breath. She let it out and smiled. It was a magical moment.

"That was incredible," she said to Hawk.

"It sure was," he agreed. They walked back to Nikki's house. When they got in, they took off their outer layers in her foyer. They carried their boots and jackets into the den and put them by the roaring fire. Hawk asked if Nikki wanted some more coffee.

"How about I make some hot chocolate?" she suggested.

"I will never say no to that," Hawk replied. Nikki made the hot chocolate while Hawk relaxed in the den. She also put a bag of marshmallows, a box of graham crackers, and some of her chocolates on a plate. She put the plate and mugs on a tray and added two skewers. She took the tray into the den.

Hawk was sitting on the floor by the fire. He saw the tray and his eyes lit up.

"S'mores," he exclaimed. "I love s'mores." Nikki smiled. She put the tray on the floor and joined Hawk. They both put marshmallows on a skewer and roasted them on the fire. When they were perfectly browned on the outside and melting on the inside, they slid the marshmallows onto the graham crackers with a piece of chocolate. They smashed another graham cracker on top and ate them. A little while later, Nikki was licking marshmallow off her fingers and sipping hot chocolate. Hawk was leaning back, watching her. He smiled.

"This is so relaxing. I am glad Lidia made me take the day off," Nikki said.

"So am I," said Hawk. There was a silence as they both contemplated the long, stressful week that had led up to this beautiful, peaceful day.

"Do you think he is doing the right thing?" Nikki looked at Hawk.

"Who?" asked Hawk, confused.

"Seth. I know he wants to get into law enforcement, but after yesterday, I worry something will happen to him." Hawk moved over and put his arm around her.

"I understand you are worried. I am worried, too. But Seth is an intelligent young man. He will not put himself into any danger he cannot handle. I am sure of that. Remember yesterday when we told him to wait with the chief?" Nikki nodded. Hawk continued, "He did. If he had not waited and insisted on going into the building with us, I would be concerned."

"You are right," Nikki agreed. "He did listen. I still just think of him as my baby boy sometimes. It is hard to watch him grow up so fast. Pretty soon he will move out and have a family of his own."

"Yeah, and then you will be a grandma." Hawk ducked as Nikki threw a punch at him. They laughed.

"You know I will make sure he has the best training possible," Hawk reassured Nikki.

"I know, and thank you. That means a lot to me."

Hawk sat up and took Nikki's hand. "I have something for you," he said. He pulled a narrow rectangular box out of his pocket, wrapped in red paper. He handed it to Nikki. Nikki smiled.

"Thank you," she said and pulled off the wrapping. She opened the box and her breath left her. It was a gorgeous gold necklace with a heart locket. It had flowers carved in tiny filigree, and a tiny diamond star sparkling in the center. She gasped. "Is this…"

"Yes. It's the locket you saw at the antique store. I knew it had to be yours. Just like the one your mother had."

Nikki opened the locket. There was a picture of Seth. Nikki felt the tears forming. She looked at Hawk. He smiled. She kissed him and thanked him again.

"I want you to always have Seth right by your heart," he said.

Nikki wiped a tear away. "He is not the only one who should be in here," she said. Hawk looked at her quizzically. "I need your picture here, too. I always want you close to my heart." Hawk swept her in his arms and kissed her. She hugged him close, happy to be with the man that she loved.

more from wendy

about wendy meadows

Wendy Meadows is a USA Today bestselling author whose stories showcase women sleuths. To date, she has published dozens of books, which include her popular Sweetfern Harbor series, Sweet Peach Bakery series, and Alaska Cozy series, to name a few. She lives in the "Granite State" with her husband, two sons, two mini pigs and a lovable Labradoodle.

Join Wendy's newsletter to stay up-to-date with new releases. As a subscriber, you'll also get BLACKVINE MANOR, the complete series, for FREE!

Join Wendy's Newsletter Here
wendymeadows.com/cozy